VISITATION

JENNY ERPENBECK was born in East Berlin in 1967. She learned bookbinding, studied theatre sciences and worked backstage at the Staatsoper theatre in Berlin before becoming an opera director, playwright and writer. Her fiction has been translated worldwide, and her novel *The Old Child* was awarded one of Germany's Aspekte Prizes for Literature.

SUSAN BERNOFSKY has translated works by Robert Walser, Hermann Hesse, Gregor von Rezzori, Yoko Tawada, Ludwig Harig and Peter Szondi. She is the author of *Foreign Words: Translator-Authors in the Age of Goethe* and is currently at work on a biography of Robert Walser. Her translation of *The Old Child and Other Stories* was awarded the 2006 Helen and Kurt Wolff Translator's Prize.

VISITATION

JENNY ERPENBECK

TRANSLATED FROM THE GERMAN
BY SUSAN BERNOFSKY

Portobello
BOOKS

Published by Portobello Books Ltd 2010

Portobello Books Ltd
12 Addison Avenue
London W11 4QR

Copyright © Eichborn Verlag, Frankfurt am Main 2008
Translation copyright © Susan Bernofsky 2010

Originally published by Eichborn Verlag, Frankfurt am Main, 2008,
under the title *Heimsuchung*.

The translation of this work was supported by a grant from the
Goethe-Institut, which is funded by the German Ministry of Foreign
Affairs.

The short quotation by Friedrich Hölderlin on p. v is Nick Hoff's
translation as it appears in *Odes and Elegies* (Wesleyan, 2008).

A CIP catalogue record is available from the British Library

2 4 6 8 9 7 5 3 1

ISBN 978 1 84627 189 2

www.portobellobooks.com

Offset by Avon DataSet Ltd, Bidford on Avon, Warwickshire

Printed and bound in the UK by JF Print Ltd., Sparkford, Somerset

For Doris Kaplan

As the day is long and the world is old, many
people can stand in the same place, one after the other.

—*Marie in* Woyzeck, *by Georg Büchner*

If I came to you,
O woods of my youth, could you
Promise me peace once again?

—*Friedrich Hölderlin*

When the house is finished, Death enters.

—*Arabic proverb*

PROLOGUE

APPROXIMATELY TWENTY-FOUR THOUSAND *years ago, a glacier advanced until it reached a large outcropping of rock that now is nothing more than a gentle hill above where the house stands. The enormous pressure exerted by the ice snapped and crushed the frozen trunks of the oaks, alders and pines that grew there, sections of rock broke away, splintered and were ground to bits, and lions, cheetahs and saber-toothed cats fled to more southerly climes. But the ice did not advance beyond this rocky crag. Gradually silence set in, and the ice began its labor, a labor of sleep. While over a period of millennia it stretched out or shifted its enormous cold body only a centimeter at a time, it gradually was polishing the rocky surface beneath until it was round and smooth. During warmer years, decades and centuries, the water on the surface of the block of ice melted a little, and in places where the sand beneath the ice was easy to wash away, the water slipped beneath the huge, heavy ice body. And so at the very spot where this rocky elevation had hindered the ice's forward motion, the ice slid beneath itself in the form of water and thus began to retreat, flowing downhill. In colder years the ice was simply there, it lay where it was, a heavy weight. And where in warmer years it had carved channels in the ground as it melted, during the colder years, decades and centuries it pressed its ice into these channels with all its force to seal them up again.*

•

When approximately eighteen thousand years ago the glacier's tongues began to melt—soon followed, as the earth continued to grow warmer, by all its southernmost limbs—it left only a few deposits behind in the depths of their channels, islands of ice, orphaned ice; later they were called dead ice.

Cut off from the body it had once belonged to and trapped in these channels, this ice melted only much later. Approximately thirteen thousand years before the start of the Common Era, it turned back into water, seeped into the earth, evaporated in the air and then rained back down again, circulating in the form of water between heaven and earth. When it could not penetrate any deeper because the ground was already saturated, it collected on top of the blue clay and rose up, its surface cutting through the dark earth, and now it became visible again within its channel as a clear lake. The sand that the water itself had ground from the rock when it was still ice now slid into this lake and sank to the bottom, and so at several points underwater mountains were formed, while in other spots the water remained as deep as the channel itself had originally been. For a time this lake would hold up its mirror to the sky amid the Brandenburg hills, it would lie smooth between the oaks, alders and pines that were growing once more, and much later, after human beings appeared, it was given a name by them: Märkisches Meer, the Sea of the Mark Brandenburg; but one day it would vanish again, since, like every lake, it too was only temporary—like every hollow shape, this channel existed only to be filled in completely some day. Even in the Sahara there was water once. Only in modern times did something come about there that is described in the language of science as desertification.

THE GARDENER

NO ONE IN THE VILLAGE knows where he comes from. Perhaps he was always here. He helps the farmers propagate their fruit trees in the spring, inoculating the wild stock with active buds around Midsummer's Day and dormant ones when the sap rises for the second time, he grafts new scions onto the trees chosen for propagation using whip or cleft grafts depending on the thickness of the stock, he prepares the required mixture of wax, turpentine and resin, then bandages each wound with raffia or paper, everyone in the village knows that the trees propagated by him display the most regular crowns as they continue to grow. During the summer the farmers hire him as a reaper and to build the shocks. And when the time comes to drain the dark earth of the parcels of land along the lake, his advice is eagerly sought, for he knows how to weave green spruce twigs into braids and place them in the boreholes to the proper depth to draw out the water. He helps the villagers repair their harrows and plows, lends a hand cutting wood in the winter and then saws up the trunks. He himself owns no land, not even a patch of forest, he lives alone in an abandoned hunting lodge at the edge of the woods, he's always lived there, everyone in the village knows him, and yet he is only ever referred to by both young people and old as The Gardener, as though he had no other name.

THE WEALTHY FARMER
AND HIS FOUR DAUGHTERS

WHEN A WOMAN gets married, she must not sew her own dress. The dress may not even be made in the house where she lives. It must be sewn elsewhere, and during the sewing a needle must not be broken. The fabric for a wedding dress may not be ripped, it must be cut with scissors. If an error is made while the fabric is being cut, this piece of fabric may no longer be used, instead a new piece of the same material must be purchased. The shoes for the wedding may not be a gift from the bridegroom, the bride must purchase them herself, and she must do so using the pennies she has saved over the course of many months. The wedding may not take place during the hottest time of year, that is, the dog days of summer, nor may it be held during the inconstant month of April; the weeks in which the banns are published may not overlap with the week of martyrdom before Easter, and the wedding itself must take place on the night of a full moon or at least a waxing moon; the best month for a wedding is May. Several weeks before the date of the wedding, the banns are announced and a notice posted in the display case outside the church. The bride's girlfriends twine flowers into garlands with which they encircle the display case. If the girl is popular in the village, there will be three or more garlands. One week before the wedding day, the slaughtering and baking begins, but the bride must not under any circumstances glimpse a fire flickering in the cook stove. The day before the wedding, the children of the village come in the afternoon and make a racket, they throw crockery in front of the gate of the house so that it breaks, but never glass, and are served cake by the bride's mother. On the eve of the wedding, the adults bring their gifts, they recite poems and partake of the pre-wedding feast. On the eve of a wedding, the lamps may not flicker, that brings bad luck. The next morning the bride sweeps up the shards from before the gate and throws them into a pit the bridegroom has dug. After this, the bride is adorned by her friends for the wedding ceremony, she wears a myrtle wreath and veil. When the bride and groom come out of the house, two girls are holding up a garland of flowers that they lower so that the bride and groom can step over it. At once they must be driven to the church. The horses wear two ribbons on the outer edges of their bridles, red for love and green for hope. The whips display the same ribbons. The bridal carriage is adorned with a festoon of boxwood or sometimes juniper. The bridal carriage is the last in the procession, it follows the carriages of the guests and must not stop or turn around. The bridal procession must avoid, if at all possible, driving past a cemetery. The bride and groom must look straight ahead during the ride. If it rains, this is all right, but it must not snow during the ride. For every flake of snow / Another tale of woe. Further the bride must not drop her handkerchief at the altar or there will be many tears in the marriage. On the way home, the carriage of the bride and groom precedes all the others, it must travel quickly or else the marriage itself will not move forward as it should. When the bride and groom cross the threshold of the bride's home, they must step over something made of iron, such as an axe or a horseshoe. During the wedding feast, the bride and groom sit in a corner, the bridal corner, which they must not leave. The chairs of the bride and groom are adorned with tendrils of ivy. After the meal, a boy sneaks under the table and pulls off one of the bride's shoes, which is then auctioned off and in the end must be won at auction by the groom.

The proceeds go to the women who cooked the meal. At twelve midnight, the bride's veil is torn to pieces while songs are sung, and each guest receives a piece of the veil as a memento. After the wedding, the young couple moves into their new lodgings. Good friends have placed a little package containing bread, salt and a bit of money on the stove so that they will never be lacking sustenance and money. The package must remain lying there undisturbed for one year. The two words that are most important for a wedding are: may and must, and may, and must, and may, and must. The first task the young wife must perform in the new lodgings is fetching water.

The village mayor has four daughters: Grete, Hedwig, Emma and Klara. On Sundays, when he drives his daughters through the village in his carriage, he puts white stockings on the horses. The father of the mayor was mayor before him, and the father's father was mayor, and the father of his father's father and so on, all the way back to the year 1650. The king himself appointed as mayor the father of the father of the father of the mayor's father, and this is why when the mayor drives through the village on Sundays in a carriage filled with daughters, he puts white stockings on the horses. Grete, Hedwig, Emma and Klara sit in the carriage that their father is driving himself, the horses going along at an easy trot, and when the earth is still damp, they don't even get as far as the butcher shop before the horses' white stockings are flecked with mud. Sunday after Sunday when services are finished the father drives his four daughters from Kirchweg, which runs beside the church, down to Hauptstrasse, which passes the butcher shop, the school and the brickyard, and after the brickyard he turns off the main road, taking a left on Uferweg, which runs along the shore, following it north all the way to the property halfway up the Schäferberg that everyone in the village refers to as Klara's Wood because it is her inheritance. Here the girl's father turns the carriage around, and while he is turning, the girls quickly jump down in summer to pick a few raspberries on the right-hand side of the road, but

Wurrach, as the father of the four daughters is known in the village, cracks his whip as soon as he's gotten the carriage turned around, just as he is in the habit of doing on workdays when he races through the village with his empty carriage, summoning his laborers and dairymaids to work, and as soon as the father, old Wurrach, has cracked his whip, the four sisters leap back to their seats in the carriage, and now they are on their way home again, past the brickyard, school and butcher shop to the other end of the village, down to the Klotthof farm that their father inherited from his father, and his father from his father before him, and his father from his father before him and so on and so forth, the Klotthof farm that the king gave Wurrach's forebear as a fiefdom around 1650, along with several fields.

If a maiden wishes to know if she will marry soon, she must knock on the wall of the chicken coop during the night of New Year's Eve. If the first creature to emerge is a hen, she's out of luck, but if the rooster responds first, her wish will be granted. On New Year's Eve she can force her future husband to appear to her. If the girl wishes to marry a boatman, she must sit down on a wheelbarrow, and the one she longs for will soon appear. To wed a mason, she must take a seat upon a chopping block. If she then takes up a mortar box and a mason's trowel, he will soon arrive. If she wants a farmer, she must hold a scythe and a spade. The mother of a marriageable daughter is eager to lure suitors to her home. She can do so by intentionally allowing the cobwebs to remain hanging in the sitting room. If the cobwebs are destroyed, any suitor will be taken away.

The mother of the four girls died giving birth to Klara. The mayor has no son. There are smallholders and cottagers in the village, two cottiers and a few farmers, but only a single village mayor.

Grete does not marry, because the oldest son of the farmer Sandke with whom she was betrothed, the only one of the six Sandke sons who received agricultural training, because he was to inherit the Sandke farm, learned just before the wedding, both to his own astonishment and that of his father, that the landowner did not choose him to inherit the property. Because of this, the wedding is deferred, and after a brother-in-law of the landowner does in fact take over the farm the following September, Grete's betrothed boards a steamer in Bremerhaven and for 280 marks journeys by way of Antwerp, Southampton, the Strait of Gibraltar, Genoa, Port Said, the Suez Canal, the Red Sea, Aden, Colombo and Adelaide to Melbourne, Australia, where after six weeks at sea he arrives on November 16, 1892, with 8 marks to his name and a gold pocket watch that he pawns for 20 marks. From Melbourne he reports these things in a letter to his fiancée, and thereafter Grete never hears from him again, and the fields belonging to Sandke's farm that border the Wurrach property are now lost forever to the mayor's family.

Hedwig gets involved with a workman who threshes the grain on the Klotthof farm in the summer. When her father is informed of this by a neighbor, he bursts into the barn in the middle of the day, wrests the flail from the worker's hand and drives him from the farm with the words: I'll take my axe, I'll strike you dead!, he chases after him as far as the edge of the woods, and everyone in the village hears his voice, which has become huge from years of giving orders, it's gotten stretched out of shape and thus resembles the voice of a drunkard: I'll take my axe, I'll strike you dead! When he comes back to the farm, he locks Hedwig in the smokehouse up in the loft, where she loses her child, which at the time is not yet anything more than a little bloody clump.

Emma, the third oldest daughter of the mayor, would surely have made a good mayor herself if she'd been born a man. She assists her father at every turn, makes decisions in his absence about the villagers' payments, hires farmhands and maids, oversees the felling of trees and the maintenance of fields and livestock. The question of Emma's marrying someday has never been mentioned by anyone at all, neither in the family nor the village.

And now Klara, the mayor's youngest daughter, stands to inherit the bit of woods on the hill called Schäferberg. The lower edge of the woods borders the lake, and its upper edge, the meadow with the raspberry vines that belongs to the estate; on the right it extends to the property line of Old Warnack's land, and on the left borders the meadow of a smallholder who for years has been in conflict with Klara's father over illegal pasturing, as Wurrach claims this meadow as his own. Given these circumstances, Klara's Wood is seen by her father as an island that they cannot expect to combine with other properties through marriage.

When the fisherman comes ashore on her bank, Klara doesn't know what to say. The fisher lad doesn't say anything either, he just tosses her the rope, which she catches and ties around an alder tree. It's just coincidental that she happens to be in her woods today. After Hedwig's unfortunate incident, the father stopped taking his daughters for rides in the carriage. Today Klara is alone here and on foot, she picked raspberries up on the meadow and then made her way down the hill among the bushes and trees that belong to her: oaks, alders and pines, to see the water glittering, since from the Klotthof farm you can't see the lake, even in winter when the trees have lost their leaves.

The unknown fisherman holds out his hand, and she helps him climb out of the rocking boat and then lets his hand go again. Only when he holds out his hand to her a second time does she understand that he wants her to lead him further. Halfway up the slope where the earth is no longer quite so dark and the grass is drier, there will surely be a place for her and the fisherman, whose hair is so wet that the water is dripping to his shoulders and running down his arms all the way to where his fingers are intertwined with hers. Only now, when she is looking for a good spot to sit down with him, does it strike her how many people there are all around her in this bit of woods, and everywhere there might be an attractive spot to rest, someone is already sitting or standing, some are reclining in the shade, asleep, others are having their evening meal, and yet others are leaning against a tree, smoking and blowing rings in the air. It's no doubt because all these people are so quiet that she didn't notice them before. In a sunny spot under the big oak tree the kind of grass she likes is growing, tall, dry grass, tuft after tuft of it, and when she kneels down there and draws the fisherman down beside her, the others finally begin to move, they put their sandwiches, apples and hard-boiled eggs back in their baskets, fold up their blankets and calmly rise to their feet, while the ones who are leaning against the tree trunks now toss their cigarettes on the ground and crush the stubs beneath the soles of their shoes. One at a time, all of them turn to walk back up the slope, leaving behind this place without addressing a single word or even a wave to Klara and her fisherman. The fisherman lays his head in the lap of the mayor's youngest and as yet unmarried daughter, and she begins to dry his wet shock of hair with her skirt. On the far side of the oak tree directly behind her, two last silent visitors to this bit of woods whom she had overlooked now rise to their feet and leave as well.

Red is birth, / green is life, / white is death.

I know a little creaturely, / its features are quite mannerly. / Good manners has the creaturely./ It wears its bones atop its flesh.

In our cellar lies a man / who has a hundred petticoats on.

Something crosses the floor, / it doesn't tip, it doesn't tap.

Toss it up on the roof white / and it comes down yellow.

In our garden stands a white mare / whose tail reaches high into the air.

A queen was drinking tea. / Three hinds were swimming / across the lake. / What was the queen's name?

I'm a poor soldier and must stand watch, / I have no legs but have to march, / I have no arms but have to fight / and tell all the people what is right.

Nothing but holes. / And still it holds.

At first the sisters don't notice anything except that Klara is now sometimes particularly courteous when she wishes them good morning and inquires as to their well-being, as though they were strangers, or as though she hadn't seen them in a long time. On other days she might look away when her sisters wish her good morning. The second thing that strikes her sisters as well as the people in the village is that Klara often leaves the farm with the bucket of scraps intended for the hogs instead of emptying it out in the sty. With the bucket in her hand, she walks through the village, passing the butcher shop and school, and after the brickyard turns left onto Uferweg. Old Warnack, whose grounds border Klara's Wood on the right-hand side, reports to Wurrach that Klara always first empties her bucket there somewhere in the bushes and then sits down in the grass, leaning her back against the oak tree and propping her feet on the upside-down bucket, and talks with the air or else is simply silent. After her father forbids her to leave the farm, she begins to hide within the farm itself. She squats down behind the bushes and trees in the garden, or under boards that are leaning up against a wall somewhere, she also climbs into barrels and chests. Everywhere on the farm and on the property, the sisters and farmhands have to be prepared to come across Klara. She can often be heard wailing or arguing in some hiding place or other, but if you pull her out, she is always quiet and friendly. Once Grete opens the closet door to take out a broom, and Klara is standing there in the cramped space smiling at her calmly as though she had been waiting in the dark for her sister all the while. Another time she puts her hand into her bowl during lunch and in front of everyone smears the hot porridge all around her mouth as though she were intentionally resisting finding the entrance, but all this time she is smiling and appears content. For a moment everything is very still at the table of the village mayor. During this period there is scarcely a farmhand or maid willing to enter into the service of the powerful Wurrach, for it is no trivial matter to arm oneself against possible attack by someone who has veered from the world of appropriate behavior. Her sisters place all the sharp knives in a drawer with a lock, the farmhands lay their axes high up on top of the compartment built into the entry gate, which a woman cannot reach without a stepstool, and in Klara's room her father removes the window latches and the inside door handle, during the night he himself locks the door from the outside. During the night, Klara, the last daughter of the village mayor, sometimes turns her chamber pot upside down and uses it as a drum.

This is the key to the garden / for which three girls are waiting. / The first is named Binka, / the second Bibeldebinka. / The third's name is Zickzettzack Nobel de / Bobel de Bibel de Binka. / Then Binka took a stone / and struck Bibeldebinka's leg bone. / Then Zick, Zett, Zack, / Nobel de Bobel de Bibel de Binka / began to weep and to moan.

And then nothing further happens except that Grete and Hedwig and Emma and even Klara grow older, and their father grows old. Nothing further happens except that in Klara's Wood one of the old oak tree's branches breaks off, remains lying there in the grass and rots. All the villagers have long since gotten used to the Mayor's Old Maid, as Klara is now called by the villagers, sometimes limping through the village with two different shoes on her feet or perhaps only socks, walking as far as the butcher shop, the school, the brickyard but never farther, and if you ask her: Where are you going? she will reply: Dunno.

Last glove / I lost my autumn. / I had to find three days / before I looked for it. / Then I walked past a garden, / and saw a gentleman there. / Around the gentleman sat three tables. / Then I

*took off my day / and wished them all a good hat, sirs. / Then
the gentlemen laughed to begin / until their bursts bellied.*

Old Wurrach sells the first third of Klara's Wood to a coffee and
tea importer from Frankfurt an der Oder, the second third to
a cloth manufacturer from Guben, who enters his son's name
in the contract of sale in order to arrange for his inheritance,
and finally Wurrach sells the third third, the part where the
big oak tree stands, to an architect from Berlin who discovered this sloping shoreline with its trees and bushes while out
for a steamboat ride and wishes to build a summer cottage
there for himself and his fiancée. The village mayor enters into
conversations about so-and-so-many square meters first with
the coffee and tea importer, then with the cloth manufacturer,
and finally with the architect, for the first time in his life he is
measuring ground not in hides or hectares, for the first time
in his life he is speaking of parcels of land. For several hundred years Klara's Wood was considered logging grounds, every thirty years all the land surrounding the big oak tree was
cleared and then reforested, and now a number of the trees are
to remain there forever just as they stand, the architect's fiancée
says: For the shade. While her father is negotiating the price for
the third third, Klara, whom everyone now calls the Mayor's
Old Maid, goes limping through the village as always, one of
her feet shod, the other with just a stocking on, she limps past
the butcher shop, then past the school, then past the brickyard,
and later back again. At dusk, snow falls for the first time. As
the seller of the third parcel of land on Schäferberg, Old Wurrach signs the contract in the name of his incapacitated daughter, and on behalf of the architect, the architect's young fiancée
signs as the new landowner.

Not until the next day does Emma discover Klara's footprints
in the freshly fallen snow, down at the public bathing area they
lead directly into the gray water, always in alternation: a shoe,

a stocking, a shoe, a stocking, a shoe. Soon thereafter her body is found as well, near the shore beside the brickyard it has gotten entangled in the pine roots laid bare when the soil washed away beneath them. The pastor doesn't want to give the suicide a Christian burial, but the mayor, who has meanwhile, despite his advanced age, been chosen as the local leader of the Reich Farmers League, puts his foot down.

In a household where a death has taken place, the clock must be stopped at once. The mirror is covered with a cloth, otherwise you will see two dead people. The uppermost windows are opened, and if the roof has no dormers, one roof tile is removed so that the soul can escape. The dead person is washed and dressed. A man is dressed in a black walking coat, a woman in her black dress. The dead person's shoes are put on. A virgin is buried adorned as a bride in a white dress, myrtle wreath and veil. The dead person is placed on a bed of straw. The dead person's face is covered with a cloth soaked in brandy or vinegar. Nettles are strewn on the body to keep it from turning blue. On either side of a male corpse an axe must be placed. A female corpse has an axe placed upon her torso with the handle pointing toward her feet. When the corpses are placed in their coffins, the axes are removed. The vessel containing the water with which the corpse was washed must be buried beneath a rain spout. The straw on which the dead person lay is burned or buried together with his old clothes. The death is announced to the animals in the stable and the trees in the garden with the words: Your master is dead. Before the coffin is carried across the threshold it must be set down three times. To prevent the soul from entering the house once the coffin has crossed the threshold, all the windows and doors must be closed at once. Pour water on the floor and sweep the floors with a broom. The chairs the coffin rested on are turned upside-down on the floor. To exclude every possibility of return, water from a bowl is thrown after the funeral procession as it moves away, just as one does when the doctor or knacker leaves the farm.

THE GARDENER

WHEN THE FIRST VACATION homes are built on the shores of the lake, many of them with thatched roofs, the gardener helps cut the reeds for the roofs as soon as the lake freezes over, and here too he proves unusually deft, the frozen stems crack like glass before him, he manipulates the board used to transport the stalks so skillfully that the roofer finds it difficult to believe he has never before helped out during the reed harvest. With great vigor he pounds the stalks across his left knee without ever growing weary, the short pieces and bits of grass fall to the ground straightaway, then he lays the neat bundles off to the side.

The gardener doesn't speak much, and he's never been heard to say anything at all about events in the village, whether someone has drowned in the lake, a smallholder has secretly changed the position of a border stone, or Schmeling has knocked out the American boxer Louis in the twelfth round. That's our Schmeling, the roofer says from his perch high up on the thatching stool down to where the gardener is handing him the bundles of reeds, our Schmeling going up against the Brown Bomber, that was something, or don't you have a radio? The gardener shakes his head. The house upon whose roof the roofer is currently sitting belongs to Schmeling. I put the roof on the Thorak place too, the roofer told the gardener when they were first beginning to work together, perhaps in the hope of impressing the gardener,

15

who was known for being taciturn, and moving him to speak, but probably the gardener didn't even know who Thorak was, and in any case his only response had been a silent nod.

Many in the village find the gardener's silence unsettling, they declare him cold, call the expression in his eyes fishy, suspect his high forehead of harboring traces of madness. Some, on the other hand, point out that while his communications with others are kept to a minimum, when he thinks he is alone in a garden or field, they've clearly seen him moving his lips constantly as he hoes, digs, weeds and prunes or waters plants—in other words, he prefers talking with vegetables. No one is admitted into his hut, and children who peek through the window when he isn't home see only a table, chair, bed and a few items of clothing that have been tossed over hooks. So the hut, too, is silent, just like its owner, and as is always the case with silences, this might indicate that it is hiding a secret, or else simply that it is empty through and through.

When the thatch roof on the house that a Berlin architect is having built for himself and his wife on Klara Wurrach's land is already almost finished—the roofer and the gardener are just taking a break before they incorporate the last bundles of reeds into the roof—the householder-to-be joins them and asks the two villagers whether they might know someone in the area who could help transform the woods into a garden. And as is to be expected, the roofer recommends the gardener who is sitting right beside him and continues to maintain his silence but then, by giving the architect a brief nod, he indicates his assent.

The landscape architect, a cousin of the householder who resides in the nearby spa town, now comes by on a daily basis to discuss the plans with the householder and gardener and oversee the work. On the flat upper stretch of land between house and lake, the pine forest is to be cleared away and topsoil added so that the lawn will take root well. The smaller part of the meadow on the left-hand side, directly in front of the house, is to be ringed with evergreens and elderberry, and only a rose-bed will separate it from the terrace.

The boundary of the larger part of the meadow, to the right of the path that leads down to the water, will be defined in back by the wooden fence running between it and the next-door property, which is still in its natural state, the edge facing the hill by the big oak tree and a grouping of fir shrubs, the edge nearest the house by forsythia, lilac and a few rhododendrons, and the edge fronting the sandy road by shrubs planted along the row of fieldstones marking the border of the property.

The addition of a few new trees will contribute to the impression of a natural gradation: a hawthorn at the edge of the meadow to the left, and on the meadow to the right a Japanese cherry, a walnut and a blue spruce—in each case placed so as to lead up to the bushes or the larger trees already standing in the background.

To supplement the pines, the young oak saplings and the little hazelnut shrubs that grow naturally on the slope leading down to the lake, additional bushes will be planted close together to make it more stable.

A path paved with broken flagstones leading down the slope in eight times eight steps will provide access to the lake.

Since the patch of land down near the water is particularly shady and damp thanks to the alders that grow along the shore, the landscape architect in consultation with the householder instructs the gardener to fell several of the trees there and drain the land along the shoreline. In order to make the most of this spot, which isn't terribly inviting, the householder decides to have a workshop and a woodshed built there according to his own specifications. Later it can be established where a good place will be to build a dock.

·

Each of the two upper meadows with its natural frame will become an arena, the landscape architect says to his cousin, the householder, while the gardener is dumping out a wheelbarrow full of compost-rich soil on the site of the future rose-bed in front of the terrace. The householder says: Basically it's always just a matter of framing the view. And providing variety, the landscape architect says: light and shade, open spaces and thickly overgrown ones, looking down from above, looking up from below. With the edge of his shovel, the gardener distributes the soil evenly across the bed. The vertical and the horizontal must stand in a salutary relationship to one another, the householder says. Precisely, says the landscape architect, and that's why this naturally cascading slope leading down to the water is ideal. The gardener wheels the empty barrow away. The two men stand on the terrace and from this vantage point gaze down at the lake, which is gleaming and sparkling between the reddish trunks of the pines. The gardener wheels up the next barrowful of soil and dumps it out. To tame the wilderness and then make it intersect with culture—that's what art is, the householder says. Precisely, says his cousin, nodding. With the edge of his shovel, the gardener distributes the soil evenly across the bed. To avail oneself of beauty regardless of where one finds it, the owner says. Precisely. The gardener wheels his empty barrow past the two men standing on the terrace, both of them now silent.

And so the gardener fells several pine trees, saws them up and stacks the wood in the woodshed, he clears the roots and spreads a generous layer of topsoil over the Brandenburg sand, the gardener lays the path between the small and large meadows, and then extends it down the hill, eight times eight steps made of natural sandstone, he sows grass, plants the roses, plants shrubs to frame the small and large meadows, plants bushes on the slope, sets out hawthorn, walnut, Japanese cherry and blue spruce, as he digs he works his way through a thin layer of humus and then strikes bedrock that has to be broken up with the spade, for only beneath this is the layer of sand with the groundwater coursing through it, and finally beneath this sand is the blue clay that is found everywhere in this region. Once upon a time the waters of the lake washed over this rise that is called the Schäferberg or Shepherd's Mountain by the locals, and thousands of years ago the Schäferberg was nothing but a shoal beneath the surface of the water, just as the Gurkenberg is today, or the Black Horn, the Keperling, the Hoffte, the Bulzenberg, the Nackliger, whose name means "naked man," or Mindach's Hill. The layer of sand beneath the bedrock that the gardener uncovers when he is digging his holes still displays a wave-like pattern, immortalizing the winds that blew across the water long ago. The gardener excavates the holes for the plants up to a depth of 80 centimeters and fills the bottom with composted soil so that the shrubs, bushes, Japanese cherry, hawthorn, blue spruce and walnut will flourish. Down beside the shore of the lake the gardener chops down five alder trees, clears the roots, braids green spruce twigs and places them in the boreholes so the black earth at the bottom will dry out. The gardener waters the roses, shrubs and young trees twice a day during the summer, once early in the morning and once at dusk, and he continues to water the bare soil of both meadows until the grass begins to sprout.

The gardener prunes all the bushes that overhang the stone perimeter in the fall, and prunes the forsythia and lilac the following spring as soon as they have blossomed. He removes the weeds from between the roses, prunes the roses, and has the farmers give him cattle dung that he uses to fertilize the hawthorn, walnut and Japanese cherry as well as the forsythia, lilac and rhododendron; he waters the roses and bushes twice a day during the summer, once early in the morning and once at dusk, on each of the meadows he places a sprinkler that bows to one side and then the other for half an hour twice a day, once early in the morning, and once when dusk is already beginning to gather, the gardener mows the grass once every two or three weeks. In fall, he saws the dry branches from the big trees with a long saw and smokes out the moles, in fall he rakes up the leaves from the meadows and burns them, when fall is coming to an end he empties all the water pipes in the house and shuts off the main valve, in winter he heats the house when the architect and his wife will be arriving and turns the water back on for the length of their stay.

THE ARCHITECT

HOW BITTER IT IS that he is having to bury everything. The porcelain from Meissen, his pewter pitchers and the silver. As if it were wartime. He himself doesn't know whether he is burying something or simply laying in provisions for his return. He doesn't even know if there's any real difference between the two. In general he knows far less now than he used to. Just before the Russians marched in, his wife had packed up these very plates, these tankards and this silverware in crates, but that time she'd rowed out on the lake with the crates and lowered everything into the water on the shoal of the Nackliger which she knew from swimming. That was the place in the middle of the lake that was so shallow that when she was swimming far from shore in summer her feet would suddenly get tangled in the water plants and then she would start laughing and pretend to be drowning. The Russians, looking for what might have been hidden from them, only thought to poke around in the grass and the flowerbeds with long sticks, and while they were jabbing their sticks around, the lake was unhurriedly rinsing the dust from the treasures that were being kept safe from them. The new occupants of the house will have more time for swimming.

He's lucky the winter is so mild this year, lucky that he's able to get his spade into the earth at all. He buries his pewter pitchers among the roots of the big oak tree, the Meissen under a bushy fir, and the silver in the rose-bed right next to the house. Rest in peace. He knows that two hours from now he'll be sitting in the S-Bahn to West Berlin, his fingernails still rimmed black with dirt. The architect fills up the holes, wondering whether pewter pitchers will now sprout from the buried pewter pitchers, plates and cups from the plates and cups, and forks, knives and spoons from the forks, knives and spoons, shooting up between the roses. He considers whether he shouldn't finish up by burying the spade as well and use his bare hands to cover this final pit. And finds that he no longer knows something he once used to know: what counts as valuable and what does not. Will finding his Meissen porcelain again when he returns—if he returns—really make him any happier than finding this spade worth 2 marks 50 whose wooden handle has been polished smooth by the hands of the gardener over the past twenty years? But a wooden handle like this would be eaten by worms in any case. And so he doesn't bury it, he brings it, as usual, back down to the toolshed beside the water, where for the past twenty years the spade has occupied its place among hoes, rakes, picks and shovels. Locks the toolshed, the golden spoon lure he once fished with dangling from the key, walks back up the shallow stone steps, hangs the key on the key hook in the living room, rinses his hands in the bathroom, two hours from now he'll be sitting in the S-Bahn to West Berlin, his fingernails still rimmed black with dirt, he draws the crank for the shutters out of its niche in the wall one last time and closes the shutters from inside by means of the hidden mechanism he himself once thought up as a young man, to make his wife laugh.

He walks once more up the stairs, which creak at the second, seventh and second-to-last step, passing his wife's room from which emanates, as always, the smell of peppermint and camphor; the way to his studio leads him through the crepuscular room lined with cabinets, he'd built a small window there, semicircular, shaded like an eye by the straw roof, it wasn't long ago that a marten appeared to him at this window. The marten looked through the eye into the house just as he himself was looking out through the eye, animal and man both frozen there for a moment, and then the creature flitted away. The panes of frosted glass he'd had mounted in a frame of two times three panels in the door to his studio clink softly one last time as he approaches, he opens the door and enters, stands for a moment behind his drawing table and gazes down at the lake, the table is still covered with drawings for his first building in the Berlin city center, the most important commission in his life as an architect, the commission that has now caused his downfall. In the beams he hears the martens scrabbling. The martens are staying here.

He walks back down the stairs, on the way down they creak at the second, fifteenth and second-to-last step; he himself whittled grape leaves and clusters of their fruit on the finial at the bottom of the banister. Lock the door. In his trouser pocket the key is jingling that can open and close all the doors of the house including the apiary and woodshed, Zeiss Ikon, a key meeting the highest safety standards, quality German workmanship. Lock the door. And then crossing the living room, the light-colored slabs of sandstone beneath his footsteps in the entryway, fifty-by-fifty centimeters—the handle of the door to the vestibule made of brass, flat on top to sit well in the palm, edges grooved to offer traction to the thumb, when he depresses this handle it emits, as always, a faint metallic sigh—the slabs of sandstone beneath his footsteps in the entryway thirty-by-thirty centimeters; the birds on the door of the broom closet are flying, they've been flying there for a century, the flowers have been blossoming for a century, more grapes are hanging down, the Garden of Eden in twelve square chapters; he'd salvaged the door from an old farmhouse, its beauty makes you forget entirely about the scrub-brush, broom, bucket, dustpan and brush it conceals. Frame the view, that's what he's always thought, lead the eye. In the kitchen a faucet is dripping, shut it off. Look out through the bulls-eye panes at the sandy road and trees. The colored glass turns even the bare trees green, frame the view, it's the first day of the new year, the gardener is still asleep, no one is out for a walk. Happy new year. In two hours he'll be sitting in the S-Bahn to West Berlin.

Lock the door. Lock the door and leave the key in the lock. He doesn't want them to break any of his bones. Doesn't want them to break down the door, twist off or saw apart the ironwork protecting the glass of the front door, this ironwork is painted red and black, just like the ironwork of the National Glider School that he worked on before the war, which was blown up just after the war ended, no one knew why. Lock the door.

His profession used to encompass three dimensions, height, width and depth, it was always his business to build things high, wide and deep, but now the forth dimension has caught up with him: time, which is now expelling him from house and home. We won't be doing any arresting over the weekend, the official said and let him go, meaning that he wasn't going to be killed, he was just supposed to leave, get out, scram, make himself scarce, go to the devil: In two hours he'll be sitting in the S-Bahn that will bring him to West Berlin. Five years at least, the official said, for the ton of screws he bought with his own money in the West to be used in the East, a ton of brass screws for the most important building of his life: on Friedrichstrasse in Berlin-Mitte. A building for the state that is now driving him out. He knows much less than he used to.

That's his profession: planning homes, planning a homeland. Four walls around a block of air, wresting a block of air from amid all that burgeoning, billowing matter with claws of stone, pinning it down. Home. A house is your third skin, after the skin made of flesh and clothing. Homestead. A house made to measure according to the needs of its master. Eating, cooking, sleeping, bathing, defecating, children, guests, car, garden. Calculating all these whethers, all these thises and thats, in wood, stone, glass, straw and iron. Setting out courses for lives, flooring beneath feet for corridors, vistas for eyes, doors for silence. And this here was his house. For the sitting to be done by his wife and himself, he designed the two chairs with leather cushions, for observing the sunset, he made the terrace with its view of the lake, and their shared pleasure at receiving guests had taken shape as a long table in the main room, the chill he and she felt in winter would be combated by the tiled heating stove from Holland, his and her weariness after ice-skating by the bench beside the stove, and finally his drawing at the drafting table was provided for, as it were, by the studio. And now he had to consider himself lucky he was escaping with his life, suffering his third skin to be stripped from him and fleeing, insides glisteningly exposed, to the safety of the West.

When over the enemy's lines never forget your own line of retreat. Even in the first war this was easier said than done. They'd been able to discharge their bombs over Paris, but then the airship was struck and gradually lost altitude until finally it settled on the roof of a stable in a Belgian village, burying its own gondola beneath the huge limp sack. When he and his comrades worked their way out from beneath the cloth, they saw a few chickens pecking at the sand down below in the yard, saw a cat sleeping in the sun, and only when the farmers refrained from shooting at him and his comrades but instead fetched a ladder did they know that the village had already been occupied by the Germans. And so it was pure chance that instead of being shot they were invited to climb down a Belgian ladder back into life. From the airship you gazed down at the world as if at a floor plan, but it wasn't so easy to see where the front was from so high above. To them, the village they owed their life to was occupied territory; to the Belgians, it was home, and quite possibly the front ran right between the whiskers of the sleeping cat. The lesson he learned that day was never to take a risk on so close a call.

He walks around the house to the left, passing the rhododendrons, beneath his feet the gratings with which he covered all the basement windows during the second war. The words "Mannesmann Air Raid Defense" are stamped on these gratings, even now, in the middle of peacetime. By the time the second war came along, he was already too old to be sent into battle, but in his own way he'd expanded his occupied territory. *Rule number one for aerial battle: When you attack, keep the sun behind you.*

In the morning the sunlight grazed the tops of the pine trees before the house, this meant that the weather would be lovely all day long, the terrace still lay in the shade of the house, and the butter on the breakfast table hadn't yet begun to melt. All day long, the sun shone on the two meadows to the right and left of the path that led down to the water, the sisters of his wife lay and sat there with their children in the grass playing, sleeping or reading, sunlight spotted the path as it descended amid oak leaves, conifers and hazelnut bushes down to the paved steps, eight times eight, rough sandstone in its natural color; down beside the lake the sunlight pierced the alder foliage only at intervals to reach the black earth of the shoreline, which was still moist, and the closer you came to the glistening surface of the lake, the louder the leaves rustled, the shadier it was all around you—blackout shades, Mannesmann Air Raid Defense—but all of this only in order to blind him, a summer visitor taking his first step out onto the dock, between sunlight and water he would walk toward the end of the dock, and apart from him, the one walking there, nothing else remained that might have cast a shadow. Here the sun unleashed its force, falling upon both him and the lake, and the lake threw its reflection right back up at the sun, and he, who was now sitting or lying at the end of the dock, observed this exchange, casually extracting from his hand a splinter he'd gotten when he sat or lay down, smelled the pine tar used to impregnate the wood, heard the boat plashing in the boathouse, the chain it was bound with faintly clinking, he saw fish suspended in the bright water, crabs crawling, felt the warm boards beneath his feet, his legs, his belly, smelled his own skin, lay or sat there, and since the sun was so bright he closed his eyes. And even through the blood behind his closed eyelids he saw the flickering orb.

If this bit of land, the house and the lake had not signified homeland to him, nothing would have kept him in the Eastern Zone. Now this home had become a trap. At the end of the war he had haggled and drunk with the Russians in Berlin five nights long to keep the machines from being removed from his cabinetry workshop, he had salvaged his architecture office, his business, even during the first wave of expropriations, with Socialist greetings, the rejection letter from Speer had even, in the end, gotten him the commission for the Friedrichstrasse project under the Reds, but now, six years after the end of the war, the Communists were making a grab for his business after all, this had only now occurred to them, suddenly, in the middle of peacetime—Mannesmann Air Raid Defense, *always keep your eye on your opponent*. Like children with an animal whose nature they are unable to comprehend, they were now ripping the head off this toy and would be surprised to see the thing stop twitching soon thereafter.

All his life he had worked to transform money into something real, he'd at first bought only half of this bit of land and built the house on it, later he'd added the other half with the dock and the little bathing house, his entire savings, earned by hard labor, was grounded here, it had literally put down roots as oaks, alders and pine trees, making an investment is what they used to call it, converting money into durable goods in troubled times, that's what he'd been taught, but unfortunately what he'd been taught had recently become unmoored from reality, and in the wondrous disorder that the Russians left behind for the Germans one could only pity a person who owned a piece of land and not a flying carpet.

•

Someone who builds something is affixing his life to the earth. Embodying the act of staying put is his profession. Creating an interior. Digging deeper and deeper in a place where there is nothing. From outside, the colored glass in the living room windows he's now walking past looks dull and impenetrable, the light doesn't take on life until you're sitting behind the glass, only then does it become visible as light—when it is being used. Dürer too peered through colored panes of this sort, seeing only the light of the world and not the world itself, he sat indoors creating his own world. If Dürer's wife wanted to know who was strolling about in the Nuremburg marketplace, she had to open a little flap to look down at the square. The thicker the walls and the smaller the windows, the less warmth was lost by the inhabitants of a house. Fieldstone, straw, plaster: all local materials. In the crotch marking the transition from the gabled to the side-gabled area of the roof was a small shed dormer. The house was to look as if it had just grown here like a living thing. He'd helped brick the chimney himself. He'd always gotten along well with workers and farmers. But not with this state in which one official never knew what the other was doing.

In summer he always took one last swim before leaving. Now, in January, he's taking a bath too, but not in the lake. Not even his wife would laugh at this lousy joke, though she's generally quite free with her laughter. When he will have swum here for the last time is something he no longer knows. Nor does he know whether the German language contains a verb form that can manage the trick of declaring the past the future. Maybe at some point in early September. The last time, it wasn't yet a last time, that's why he didn't take note of it. Only yesterday did it become the last time. As if time, even when you grip it firmly in your hands, can still flail and thrash about and twist which way it will. Down in the bathing house his green towel is no doubt still hanging. Perhaps someone else will use it now to dry off. When he acquired the bathing house from the Jews, their towels were still hanging there. Before it could occur to his wife to wash them, he'd gone swimming and rubbed himself dry with one of the strangers' towels. Strange towels. Cloth manufacturers, these Jews. Terrycloth. Top quality goods. Not too much to ask. His first application to join the Reichskulturkammer was turned down because on the line asking about his Aryan ancestry he had written "yes and no." *In any type of attack, it is essential to assail your opponent from behind.* Terrycloth. An official well-disposed toward him, someone he knew from school, had pointed out to him that the race of his great-grandparents was not relevant to this application, and he was then allowed to submit the application a second time, answering the Aryan question with "yes" and attaching the certificates attesting to his and his wife's ancestry as far back as their grandparents' generation, whereupon his application was accepted. The yes and the no. The gaps between the planks of the bathing house had been stuffed with oakum. All the carpentry provisional. Still, he'd paid the Jews a full half of market value for the land. And this was by no means a paltry sum. They'd never have managed to find another buyer in so short a time. Oakum. His father's mother's mother. Yes and no. By buying the property, he'd helped the Jews leave the country. No doubt they went to Africa. Or Shanghai. For better or for worse. By buying the property, he'd helped his "no" leave the questionnaire. To Africa or Shanghai, what difference did it make? Just so it was gone, done away with, gone, gone. Yes and no. *Keep the sun behind you.* Assail the sun from behind, until everything burns up, then put out the fire with the waters of the Märkisches Meer. Yes and no. With any luck the deserts in Africa and the primeval forests of China were large enough that his "no" would starve to death there, die of thirst, be eaten by wild animals. Are you of Aryan descent? Yes. So why is he having to leave now? Baron Münchhausen pulled himself out of the swamp by his own hair. But this swamp was not his homeland. The architect knows far less than he once knew. He'd dried himself off with the Jews' bath towel and then hung it back on its hook. A white terrycloth towel. Top quality goods. Later he became a member of the Reichskulturkammer. Later he received permission to build a boat shelter beside the dock. His terrycloth towel that is still hanging there is green.

He locks the gate from the outside with the spare key he's taking with him because you never know. Zeiss Ikon. Quality German workmanship. When he arrived at the crack of dawn, the handle of the gate was wet with dew. The architect now leaves the front garden through the little gate in the fence and steps onto the sandy road outside. If you start walking and then turn around again, you see the house from the front, as if you'd never been inside, you see exactly the same sight that greeted you as you arrived. He puts the key in his trouser pocket and goes over to the car. The gardener must still be asleep. Later in the day, he'll perhaps saw up the large blue spruce that got blown down the day before yesterday. But by then the owner of this blue spruce, who also owns the dirt clinging to its roots that now lie exposed, will be in West Berlin.

THE GARDENER

IN THE SPRING he puts in a flowerbed along the side of the house that faces the road, filling it at the householder's request with poppies, peonies and yellow coneflowers, with a big angel's trumpet in the middle. For the border, he just pokes a few box twigs into the earth all around the flowers, they'll put down roots and grow. In summer he sets out sprinklers on both lawns, twice each day they will bow to one side and than the other for half an hour, once early in the morning and once at dusk, meanwhile he waters the flowerbed, roses and shrubs. He cuts off the withered blooms and prunes the box tree. In the fall he harvests walnuts for the first time, coaxing the nuts from their soft husks that stain his hands brown, in the fall he gathers the dry branches that have broken off from the oaks and also a few of the pine trees during storms, he saws them into pieces, chops them up for firewood and stacks the logs in the woodshed.

By 1936, the potato beetle had already crossed the Rhine and was continuing on toward the East, in 1937 it reached the Elbe River, and now, in 1938, it is beleaguering the region around Berlin. With great patience the gardener plucks the beetles over and over from the leaves of the angel's trumpet, which as the only representative of the nightshade family in the garden has been heavily affected by this plague. He crushes the eggs of these pests and even tries to seek out and destroy their pupae by digging up the earth all around the bush. This summer the sandy road is black with beetles for days on end. At the beginning of the infestation, the leaves of the bush with its splendid red blossoms merely have holes in them and display tattered edges, but by summer's end all that remains of the bush is its skeleton, a few of the leaves' ribs and the bare main shoots of the bush itself, the blossoms having long since fallen to the ground. On instructions from the householder, the gardener removes what is left of the angel's trumpet and plants a cypress in its place as the new centerpiece for the flowerbed.

THE CLOTH MANUFACTURER

HERMINE AND ARTHUR, his parents.
   He himself, Ludwig, the firstborn.
   His sister Elisabeth, married to Ernst.
   Their daughter Doris, his niece.
   Then his wife Anna.
   And now the children: Elliot and baby Elisabeth, named for his sister.

Elliot rolls the ball to his little sister. The ball rolls across the grass, stopping in the rose-bed. Elisabeth doesn't want to retrieve it, she knows the roses will prick her, and so her brother runs over, twisting his way between the blossoms, bending them to the left and right with his elbows and using his foot to knock the ball back onto the grass. The roses are mingling their red with the deeper red of a bougainvillea growing up the wall of the house and sending its blooms arching across the living room window.

In the morning they drive east in the Adler, following the road that runs along the shore. Adler, says Arthur, the senior partner, quality German workmanship. Yes, he, Ludwig, says. They don't deliver all the way out here do they?, his father asks. Sure they do, Ludwig replies, after all, they delivered to us, didn't they? Beside him sits his mother Hermine, and in the back seat Arthur, his father, and Anna. Arthur and Hermine, Ludwig's parents, have come to visit. Two weeks later they go home again. Anna has put on her white suit in honor of her in-laws. 1 jacket and 1 skirt (Peek & Cloppenburg), acquired for purposes of emigration, early 1936, 43 marks 70.

Home. There's a commotion on the property next door, the surveyors have arrived, a few workmen and their client, an architect from Berlin. He is standing there in knickerbockers and mimes a greeting. *Heil.* Here, I'll give you a boost, says Ludwig, the uncle, to Doris, his niece. The pine tree has a sort of wooden hump around shoulder height, he lifts the child up and settles her there. So what do you see, he asks. A church tower, Doris says, pointing at the lake.

Ah, the senior partner says, what a view. Like Paradise, says Hermine, his mother. Arthur and Hermine, Ludwig's parents, have come to visit. For the photograph taken by some other vacationer, his—Ludwig's—wife Anna perches on the hood of the Adler while Hermine, his mother, leans against the little wall behind which the mountain descends steeply to the sea. His father Arthur and he are standing behind the women. The mountain range on the far side of the bay becomes a backdrop that holds the four of them together. After lunch they'll drive down to the lagoon and the beach, perhaps they'll go swimming, the waters of the Indian Ocean are gentle and warm, quite different from the western coastline where the Atlantic Ocean rages. Two weeks later Arthur and Hermine, Ludwig's parents, go home again.

I don't want to anymore, baby Elisabeth says in English and runs into the house. Elliot picks up the ball, lets it bounce a few times between his hand and the ground, and then he too goes inside. It's so warm now in the house in the middle of summer that the candles on the Christmas tree are drooping again.

Just imagine, the senior partner says, standing with his trouser legs rolled up in the warm water of the lagoon, my racing dinghy capsized this spring, right near the shore. Your father got into the water himself and helped right it again says Hermine, his mother. With rolled-up trouser legs in the Märkisches Meer. With rolled-up trouser legs in the Indian Ocean. The boy from the village who sailed it over from the boatyard was white as a sheet, his mother says. You have to keep in mind that he was under the boat for a moment. That frightened him. Arthur and Hermine, Ludwig's parents, have come to visit. Two weeks later they go home again.

Home. When it rains, you can smell the leaves in the forest and the sand. It's all so small and mild, the landscape surrounding the lake, so manageable. The leaves and the sand are so close, it's as if you might, if you wanted, pull them on over your head. And the lake always laps at the shore so gently, licking the hand you dip into it like a young dog, and the water is soft and shallow.

Ludwig named the little girl Elisabeth after his own sister. As if his sister had slid so far beneath the Earth's surface that she came out again on the other side, she slid through the entire Earth and that same year was given birth to by his wife on the other side of the world. And what about Elisabeth's, his sister's daughter Doris?

The metal of the spade scrapes past pebbles, making a sharp sound on its way into the soil. To the left, on the property next door, a foundation is being dug. *Heil.*

Elliot leaps with a single bound down the pair of steps leading out of the house onto the lawn and then ambles over to the fig tree to pick a few of its fresh fruits. Anna calls to him from the open window of the living room: Bring some back for Elisabeth too. Elliot replies in English: All right. For his children, Elliot and baby Elisabeth, he planted the fig tree and also the pineapple in the back section of the garden.

Why is there Lametta hanging on the tree, baby Elisabeth asks him, pointing at the tinsel. It's supposed to look as if the tree, der Baum, were standing in a snowy Winterwald, he replies, replies Ludwig, her father. What is a snowy Winterwald? the baby asks, Elisabeth. A deep forest, he says, in which the ground and all the branches are covered with thick Schnee, and there are icicles dangling from all the branches.

Let's wait and see how things develop, he says, says Ludwig to his father. But at least the willow will get planted today, his father, Arthur, says to him, holding out the shovel, I promised Doris. From the property next door one can hear the masons' trowels tapping against the brick. *Heil*. The owner's working right alongside them, his father says, he's not too proud to lend a hand. Ludwig digs the hole for the willow tree. The earth is black and moist so close to the water.

Always in the springtime the gardener here freshens the earth for the roses. He turns the compost and sifts it. Ludwig himself prunes the rosebushes. Céleste and New Dawn, they flourish here better than anywhere else in the world, because there is never frost. What splendid roses, his mother says, Hermine. Arthur and Hermine, Ludwig's parents, have come to visit. A week and a half later they go home again. And make sure to leave the outward facing buds when you prune, his mother says, Hermine. I know, he says, Ludwig, and pours out more tea. 1 tea service (made by Rosenthal), purchased in 1932 for 37 marks 80.

The coffee and tea importer on the other side is laying his foundation already, says Arthur, his father. Ludwig is digging the hole for the willow tree. Same architect, says his mother: your neighbor on the left. He's helping brick up the chimney himself, I saw him up there before, says Arthur, Ludwig's father, he's a good man. All Anna wants right now is a dock and a bathing house, says Ludwig, and then we'll see how things go. The workers on the property to the right exchange shouts. That's got to be enough, says Ludwig, thrusting the spade into the

ground beside the pit. His father is gazing at the quietly plashing Märkisches Meer. Home. This is your inheritance, his father says to him. I know, he, Ludwig, says, his father's only son.

The eucalyptus trees rustle louder than any other tree Ludwig
has ever heard, their rustling is louder than that of beeches, lin-
dens or birches, louder than the pines, oaks and alders. Ludwig
loves this rustling, and for this reason he always sits down to
rest with Anna and the children in the shade of these massive,
scaly trees whenever the opportunity presents itself, just to hear
the wind getting caught amid their millions of silvery leaves.

Arthur, father of Ludwig and Elisabeth, grandfather of Doris,
raises the slender trunk from the ground, places it in the hole,
calls Doris over and says to her: Hold this! Doris balances from
the edge of the hole, holding onto the little trunk with both
hands. Home. The women come closer. Anna is carrying Doris's shoes in her hand, Elisabeth says to Ludwig: How lovely
it's going to be here. Quite, Ludwig says.

Between the excoriated trunks of the tall trees, monkeys are
leaping about. The strongest of them are allowed to take their
share of the booty before the others. If you feed them, they'll
think you're weaker than they are and attack you violently
when you stop giving them food or aren't quick enough about
it. Just stop calmly where you are and walk backward. Into the
car, Ludwig says to Elliot and Elisabeth. Anna says: And leave
the windows rolled up.

Arthur says to him, Ludwig, his son: Let me take a turn, and
he picks up the spade himself and tosses the earth back into the
hole all around the root ball. Ludwig places his arm around
Anna, his future wife, and the two of them look at the broad,
glittering surface of the lake. Home. Why does everyone like
looking at the water so much, Doris asks. I don't know, Anna

replies. Doris says, maybe because there's so much empty sky above a lake, because everyone likes to see nothing sometimes. You can let go now, Arthur says to Doris.

The eucalyptus trees dry out the ground all the way down, they rob all the other plants of water. And after every forest fire, it is their seeds that are the first to sprout, crowding out all other growth. By regularly shedding its dry branches, the eucalyptus saves water and encourages the development of the fires that are so beneficial not to the individual tree but to the distribution of the species as a whole. Thanks to the high oil content of its wood, its trunks are quicker to catch fire than other trees. Between the regrown trunks, the forest floor is bare, the earth burned reddish by the blaze. The leaves of the eucalyptus trees rustle louder than those of any other tree Ludwig has ever heard.

When the willow tree has grown up tall and can tickle the fish with its hair, you'll still be coming here to visit your cousins, and you'll remember the day you helped plant it, grandmother Hermine says to little Doris. My cousins? Doris asks. You never know, says Arthur and smiles at his future daughter-in-law, Anna. Hermine says: They're still swimming around in Abraham's sausage pot. Can you eat them? Doris asks. Nonsense, says Ludwig, her uncle, and says: Come give me a hand. The two of them trample the earth firm around the trunk of the tree. With one pair of big shoes, purchased in 1932 for 35 marks, and one pair of small bare feet. Home.

Elliot and baby Elisabeth are running from the stream of the sprinkler that keeps turning to one side and then the other, they let themselves be sprayed with water and then race off again. Elliot tears a leaf from the fig tree and uses it to wave the drops in Elisabeth's direction. Elisabeth tears off a leaf too and holds it in front of her face to hide from her big brother.

·

Doris picks up a few acorns and tosses them in the lake. Look, fish, she says, pointing out, for the benefit of her uncle Ludwig, the circular waves. *Petri Heil.* Tomorrow will be the topping out ceremony at the architect's.

Ludwig calls: What are you two playing over there? Baby Elisabeth holds the fig leaf before her face and whispers: The expulsion to Paradise.

Hermine and Arthur, his parents.
   He himself, Ludwig, the firstborn.
   His sister Elisabeth, married to Ernst.
   Their daughter, his niece, Doris.
   Then his wife Anna.
   And now the children: Elliot and baby Elisabeth, named for his own sister.

Doris, says Grandfather Arthur, it's time for us to go fill a bucket to water the tree so it will grow well.

Ludwig knows that because of the dry branches that frequently fall it is not without its dangers to lie down to rest in a eucalyptus grove. But he loves to hear the leaves rustle. Back home he liked to play the piano. Back home he was a cloth maker like his father. Here he has opened an auto repair shop and specializes in clutches and brakes. Here his gardener must allow an official to stick a pencil into his curly hair. The pencil stays put. Hereupon the gardener gets a big C stamped in his passport and is forbidden to enter public parks. Since he, Ludwig, arrived here he hasn't so much as touched a piano. Baby Elisabeth plays his playing here, she takes lessons and is learning quickly as if she, even before she was born, had been able to take this with her from home, something that carries no weight: music.

Tell me again what the mountains at the bottom of the lake are called, Doris asks her grandfather. What mountains, Arthur asks in response. Ludwig says, the gardener from the neighbors' on the left just told Doris about them: Gurkenberg and Black Horn, Keperling, Hoffte, the Nackliger and Bulzenberg. And Mindach's Hill. Nackliger, the girl repeats, giggling. Elisabeth says, I wish my memory were as good as my brother's. From across the way you can hear the carpenters banging, they are all but done with the attic. *Heil*. They want to put up a thatch roof, says Arthur, his father. Might not be a bad idea for your bathing house either, he says. We'll see, says Ludwig.

He and his father appraise, along with the carpenter, the place where the bathing house will stand. It is to be built ten meters from the water, not parallel to the shore but positioned at a slight angle, facing the lake as if it were a stage. On the property of the coffee and tea importer, on the right-hand side behind the fence, the brick walls of the future ground floor are already in place, with square holes for the windows and an exit door cut all the way to the ground to provide access to the planned terrace, and through these holes you can see, depending where you are standing, either the interior of the house or, looking out, the lake and trees. Ludwig folds up the plan. And inside at least a pair of bunk beds and a washstand, says his father. We'll never be spending the night here, Father, says Ludwig. Arthur says: But it won't take up much space.

With the folded-up plan Ludwig manages to smite a mosquito that has just settled on his father's arm. To the left, the banging has stopped now, on the right you can hear the scraping of the masons' trowels against naked brick. Time to call it a day. This here is your inheritance, says the senior partner. Yes, he says, Ludwig, I know, and stows the plan for the bathing house (5.5 m long, 3.8 m wide, outer wall construction: wood, roof construction: thatch), stows both the plan and the mosquito in his briefcase. On a German shelf, this mosquito, pressed flat between large quantities of paper, will outlast time and times, and one day it might even be petrified, who knows.

•

Eight iron trestles topped with flat panels, each constructed of ten boards nailed together, with one such panel between each pair of trestles, the dock is twelve meters long, painted black with pine tar so the wood will last longer. Anna picks up baby Doris before she steps onto the dock because she's afraid the child might fall in the water. Doris wraps her legs around Anna's body. *Heil.* Elisabeth says, let her be, she won't fall.

Come on, I'll put you to bed, it's still light out, that's just how it is in summer, and Elliot, he's older than you, but I don't want to, come along now, but only if you carry me, all right; baby Elisabeth wraps her legs around Anna's body, Anna carries the girl, body to body, carries this child or that. Perhaps he married Anna because he liked the way her body jutted forward to support the weight of a little girl.

When it's winter here, that means it's summer back home and vice versa. On the skat cards belonging to Ludwig's parents, Arthur and Hermine, there was always half a king on one side of the line, and a second half on the other. One might assume it would be with just the same precision that he, Ludwig, who like his father was a cloth maker, was now being mirrored at the equator, reflecting back the image of an auto mechanic. If you look at it this way, the rustling of the eucalyptus trees is just like in the song about the linden tree beside the fountain, and the water of the lake seeps through the Earth's center to become the ocean, it's not by chance we refer to it as groundwater. Elisabeth even resembles Elisabeth.

Doris says: Now the sun is going down already. Even when you are an old woman, says her grandfather Arthur, you'll still come sit here on the shore to watch the sun slipping behind the lake. Home. Why, the girl asks. Because everyone likes to watch the sun as long as possible, says Hermine, Ludwig's mother, grandmother of Doris.

•

Sometimes when you're lucky you can see the tablecloth hanging down around Table Mountain, a veil of fog that displays a pale pink tint at sunrise. He left behind the table silver but packed the Christmas tree decorations. Twelve aluminum clips to hold the candles, Christmas tree ornaments, stars made of straw, tinsel and the glass topper. Purchased in 1928 for 14 marks 70. What are icicles, his little girl asks him, Elisabeth. On that one winter day he spent at the lake, Anna, his future wife, taught his niece Doris how to ice-skate. What is snow, his little girl asks him, Elisabeth.

Hermine and Arthur, his parents.
   He himself, Ludwig, the firstborn.
   His sister Elisabeth, married to Ernst.
   Their daughter, his niece, Doris.
   Then his wife Anna.
   And now the children: Elliot and baby Elisabeth, named for his sister.

In March '36, at the end of the winter, he, Ludwig, went chasing the winter together with his future wife Anna, traveling through the Strait of Gibraltar, the coast of Europe to the right, the coast of Africa to the left. They traveled through all of this from winter to winter. Here there is no snow in winter, only rain, lots of rain, and nonetheless he feels colder here than he ever did at home. In 1937 his parents came to visit them for two weeks, his mother says, it's so nice here, and then returns home. His father says, but what a shame about your inheritance, and returns home together with Ludwig's mother. Baby Elisabeth is still far from being born yet, even Elliot isn't there yet, the two of them are still swimming around in Abraham's sausage pot. His parents came to visit. Arthur and Hermine from Guben came to visit their son Ludwig, who has emigrated to Cape Town, and now they are traveling back to Guben, going home again, from summer to summer, through the Strait of Gibraltar, to the right the coast of Africa, to the left the coast of Europe. He and his wife Anna remain standing for a while at the harbor. He doesn't say a word, and his wife doesn't say a word either.

When in 1939 Arthur and Hermine do apply for an exit visa after all, they sell Ludwig's property along with the dock and the bathing house for half its market value to the architect next door. On account of the profit he is making on this transaction, the architect pays the National Finance Authority a 6% De-Judification Gains Tax.

The proceeds from the sale, which the parents, Arthur and Hermine, are to use to pay for their passage, which Ludwig is pleading with them to do as quickly as possible, must be transferred to a frozen bank account until their passports are ready. At approximately the same time, they are forbidden to set foot in public parks. Elliot learns to walk down the three steps to the garden without holding his mother's hand. Ludwig plants, together with his gardener, whose hair is so curly that a pencil stuck into it remains there, a fig tree and the first of the three pineapple palms.

When Holland enters the war the passports for Ludwig's parents are ready, but it is no longer possible to wire the money to the steamship company. Ludwig knows that it is not without its dangers to lie down to rest beneath a eucalyptus tree. But he loves the rustling sound. Even when the gardener shakes his head the pencil does not fall out. Elliot speaks his first word: Mum. Anna is pregnant for the second time.

Two months after Arthur and Hermine get into the gas truck in Kulmhof outside of Łodz, after Arthur's eyes pop out of their sockets as he asphyxiates, and Hermine in her death throes defecates on the feet of a woman she's never seen before, all their assets, together with the assets remaining in Germany that belonged to their son, Ludwig, who has emigrated, are seized, all the frozen bank accounts dissolved and their household goods auctioned off. All the possessions of Arthur and Hermine, including the proceeds from the sale of the property beside the lake containing 1 bathing house and 1 dock, become the property of the German Reich, represented by the Reich Finance Minister.

The town is also called Moederstadt, the Mother City. Shortly before Christmas, Ernst, Ludwig's brother-in-law, the father of Doris, contracts spotted fever while performing forced labor at the autobahn construction site and dies several days later. On Easter Monday it is Elisabeth's and Doris's turn to make the trip. It's only supposed to be a short journey, Elisabeth writes to him, Ludwig, her brother, still sitting in the train. 1 letter opener, ebony with a tin handle, purchased in 1927 for 2 marks 30. Ludwig's reply from Cape Town to Warsaw takes six weeks to get there and six weeks to come back, it is returned to him unopened. Three months later baby Elisabeth is born. In the Mother City, at the most beautiful end of the world.

THE GARDENER

WHEN THE PROPERTY is expanded, the householder assigns his gardener the job of tearing down the fence and felling the pine trees on the highest part of what used to be the next-door property. The gardener saws the wood into pieces, chops it up for firewood and stacks the logs in the woodshed. He also uproots the bushes on the level clearing at the highest point of the newly acquired land and in late fall begins to dig holes for fruit trees. Five apple trees, three cherries and three pears at the householder's request. As he digs he works his way through a thin layer of humus and then strikes bedrock and breaks through it, uncovering a layer of sand with groundwater coursing through it that displays a wave-like pattern showing how, thousands of years ago, the wind blew across the lake, and finally beneath this sand is the blue clay found everywhere in the region. The gardener digs the holes to a depth of 80 centimeters and then fills them with composted earth so the fruit trees will flourish. He diverts a few pipes from the underground drainage system he had set up on the original property so the young fruit trees will receive additional water. The gardener adds topsoil and sows grass seed between the young trees. By the time the first frost arrives, grass has sprouted on the bare soil.

THE ARCHITECT'S WIFE

HAVE YOU HEARD this one? OK, here goes.

She can't help laughing all over again, even though she's told the joke many times now, she laughs, and the others are already laughing in any case, she really does like to laugh, sometimes as a child she'd *gotten stuck in her laughter,* that's what her father called it, getting stuck in laughter, as though her body were holding on to the laughter and absolutely refusing to give it up, convulsive laughter that just went on and on without her. Even her big sisters who had to take her, their little sister, everywhere they went, would laugh when she crossed her eyes and made faces or let them talk her into trying sneezing powder as healing salts for her nose or hot chilies in place of sweet peppers. She would sneeze, snort or spit, and the others would laugh. A tightrope walker is what she wanted to be, or else a lion tamer, but this she confided to no one, not even her father, *the chief mogul,* who was really chief consul, all she wanted to do was laugh and travel for the rest of her life while her sisters went on growing, got fat and had children. Unlike them, she would go on tour forever and ever. As soon as she was old enough to balance on a tightrope or start training lions, the chief mogul, who was really chief consul, recommended she take a course in stenography. Stenography, said the mogul to the lion tamer, was worth as much as six foreign languages. Stenographers and typists were in demand all over the world, the chief mogul said. Now she was sitting with her husband and a few friends out on the terrace around a big pot in which crabs were floating that she had caught herself in the lake that afternoon and then boiled until they turned red, in her hand she held a crab's pincer and was continuing to laugh. Even before the war she'd sat here like this with her husband and several of the neighbors, or else with friends, a practice she continued during the war as well, sitting out on the terrace until late at night with a view of the lake, and still she was sitting here. She would happily keep sitting here like this unto all eternity.

Before she met her husband, for whom she started working as a stenographer as soon as she completed her training, she would never have thought that one of the greatest adventures could consist in having someone marry her. At the time her husband was still married to his first wife, he possessed a family—a wife and child, as one says. For the first time in her life, weeping borrowed her body from laughter for several evenings in a row. It had taken three quarters of a year before her boss had given her a first kiss, and a further half a year followed before the two of them began to joke about a life they would live together, and then several months more before, lying in the grass beside her on one of their outings to the countryside outside Berlin, on the shore of this wide, glittering lake, he suddenly said: This is where we could live, don't you think? Not until this day did the tightrope walker understand that a person who possesses all sorts of things, including a wife and child, must first finish sitting, then get up, then begin to walk, and then much, much later work up some speed, and only then will this person be able to take a leap, if indeed he is ever able to do so, and that when a person like this leaps, he wants to land somewhere and not nowhere. Not until this day when he said to her: This is where we could live, don't you think?, and she was lying there on her back watching the pine trees sway back and forth before the blue sky—from this day on it was clear to her that he would arrive where she was only if she was willing to wait for him on this one particular bit of earth located not terribly far from Berlin. And so the young stenographer, who would have liked best to go on tour for the rest of her life, surprised herself by replying: Yes.

It then took another half a year before he really did have the contract of sale prepared and had her sign it so that when his divorce became final half the property would not go to his wife, to whom he was still married at the time, and their son. All together, things took first as long as she had imagined they would, and then twice that, so that it was as much as she could possibly endure, and finally an additional length of time beyond the point of what was endurable. When she signed the contract of sale for the property beside the lake, she was so exhausted that when her future husband used the word "sod" to refer to the piece of land, she involuntarily heard "sad" instead and couldn't help thinking back to that forlorn Berlin winter far in the past when, as a child, she had secretly leapt from the shore onto the frozen Spree River and the very piece of ice she happened to land on cracked off from the impact and began to float downstream with the current. The sliding and balancing, her feet like ice in their wet shoes and finally the grasping to catch the hands, ladders and canes being held out to her—but above all her fear that she could drift out of Berlin before anyone succeeded in rescuing her—left her so exhausted that, still dripping, she fell asleep in the arms of the man who was carrying her home to her parents.

After signing the contract of sale, the architect had indeed gotten divorced, had shortly thereafter married her and begun construction on the house. Her laughter had returned to her, and as if her husband wanted to build this laughter into the house forever, he fulfilled her every most extravagant wish: He had a little iron bird forged onto the balcony railing in front of her room, he concealed her clothes closet, fitted with a secret mechanism to open it, behind a double door; for the telephone, there was a tiny niche in the wall beside her bed, the bedding could be stowed away behind three flaps that were built into the paneling around her bed and covered with rose-colored silk, various windows in the house were set with panes of colored glass, one of the two chairs at the dining table bore his initials, the other hers, and the shutters on the ground floor could be opened and shut by means of a concealed crank in the interior of the house—when someone was walking by, how amusing it was to startle the stranger with the silent, ghostly movement of the black shutters. Like a genie at her service, he conjured up the house for her, and she laughed. That no room was provided that might some day become a nursery was accepted by both as a matter of course.

She continued to work in her husband's office in Berlin, but on weekends the two of them always drove out to the country, and since her husband was soon designing houses for one or the other neighbor who wanted to build beside the lake and then supervising the construction, they came to spend more and more time on their bit of sod, as her husband still liked to refer to this piece of land, and their circle of friends continued to grow. While they were eating crabs, one of them—sometimes he, sometimes she—would begin to tell stories, and the more practiced they became, the more effortlessly one would interrupt the other as if by chance, to deepen their guests' laughter, and the more skillfully they delivered their punch lines. Haven't we told you this one yet? How he, and then how she, how then he, and how she, how he—how surprised she was when, how she literally had thought that, and that finally he, and so really, she says, now shaking her head mutely to fill the pause guaranteed to come. Her husband adds, she interjects, he elaborates, but she really has to add that, and he agrees with her. Just before the climax she herself starts laughing in advance, then finally the punch line, and everyone laughs, they all laugh and laugh, another beer, another glass of wine, oh yes, not for me, thank you, maybe just a glass of seltzer. In this way the architect and his wife pass the time on many evenings both for themselves and for their guests.

The architect's wife who, now that she's gotten married, understands that adventure is really always just subjecting yourself to something unfamiliar, throws herself into this sedentary life with all her inborn love of movement, and the property, not least on account of its waterfront location, proves an appropriate refuge. Her sisters, both of whom have meanwhile become mothers, watch from the dock as she swims the crawl, crossing the steamer's route and then going much farther out until her swim cap is visible only as a pin-sized dot, while they themselves stay close to shore, splashing about in the shallow water with their children; her sisters like to eat crabs, but they screech when their younger sister picks up the flailing creatures by the scruff and throws them into the net with no sign of disgust; when the swing for her nieces and nephews gets tangled in a branch of the big oak tree, she is the one who at once digs fingers and toes into the furrows of the tree's bark, quickly ascending, then straddles tree limbs to slide forward to where she can release the loop of rope caught in the leaves as if it were nothing. Her older sisters and their children sleep in until the housekeeper summons them to breakfast with the gong, but she goes walking for at least an hour before breakfast, on cool mornings the handle of the big front gate is often still wet with dew when she sets out, she hikes up into the woods and then, with a view of the lake, crosses the fields to return home. Every summer her sisters visit her with their offspring to spend a few weeks on her bit of sod, they swim, eat and swap recipes, they watch their childless sister laugh and let their bodies melt in the shade as they rest after lunch, they are relaxing, people would say, but nonetheless, even though they are refraining from all strenuous activity, these women sometimes do not look at all relaxed, they look more as if they were waiting for something and finding it difficult to wait.

•

And so the years pass and are like one single year. Whether the cockchafer plague was in '37 or maybe one year later is something she can no longer say, but she can still remember the sound to this day, the noise it made when she was out for a bicycle ride with her niece, rolling over the beetles that had transformed the sandy road into a dark, teeming surface, she hasn't forgotten the cracking beneath her tires. All summers like one single summer. Whether it was '38 or '39, or perhaps even 1940 when they began to use the dock belonging to the abandoned property next door, and when her husband built the boathouse beside the dock—she's no longer sure quite when that was. Surely he hadn't built the boathouse until the next-door property already belonged to them, but when was that? Summer after summer swimming, sunbathing and picking raspberries at the edge of the woods across from the house, autumn after autumn hearing the gardener rake up the leaves in the garden, smelling him burning the musty heap, winter after winter speeding across the frozen lake on an ice yacht and afterward taking in the sail with fingers frozen red and quickly ducking into the house: warming her hands at the stove until they hurt; Easter after Easter hiding hard-cooked eggs among the first flowers for her nephews and nieces. All like a single one. Today can be today, but it might also be yesterday or twenty years ago, and her laughter is the laughter of today, of yesterday, and just as much, the laughter of twenty years ago, time appears to be at her beck and call, like a house in which she can enter now this room, now that. Have you heard this one? While she was spending her whole life laughing, her blond hair imperceptibly turned into white hair. Today or yesterday or twenty years ago she is sitting with friends around a large pot in which crabs are floating, crabs she caught herself, gripping them firmly behind the neck, and later boiled until they turned red. Eating such a crab is not so simple. First you twist the creature's head off and suck its juices, then you rip off the claws and use a tiny skewer to pull out the meat. The best part of a crab though is the meat from its tail, which is referred to as its heart. Before you can eat it, you remove the crab's entrails and lay them aside.

Humor is when you laugh all the same, she says on one of those summer evenings during one of the last twenty years while she is sucking the marrow out of one of the claws, one of their friends, a film director, has just told everyone what a hard time the make-up department has been having making Aryan actors look Semitic so they can play that irksome racketeer Ipplmeier and his vassals. But in the rushes, at least, they looked like the real thing, the director says, heaving a sigh, and her husband says: Hope springs eternal, and she says: Humor is when you laugh all the same. Humor is when you laugh all the same, she says on some other summer evening during a different one of the last twenty years, and she cracks the shell of a crab as her husband is telling friends that he must travel to the West and use his own private funds to buy screws for the young republic because it has been expressly demanded of him that he stay within the allotted budget while also completing the building he's now working on in time for the third anniversary. In the entire Eastern Zone there are no screws to be had, unbelievable, he says, and she says: Humor is when you laugh all the same. On some summer evening during one of the last twenty years her husband tells one of the guests how at the end of the war the Russians had converted the garden to a paddock for their horses, how everything had been trampled, how he had even seen the gardener cry, he says all these things, and his wife says nothing, she is just wiping her hands on a napkin, and their friend, who after all can only judge what has been said to him, now makes his contribution to the subject by repeating in his turn: Humor is when you laugh all the same, and while he is saying this, he fishes another crab out of the pot. If it had not been for that one night, that one night in the walk-in closet that her husband had designed especially for her, she might perhaps still believe that when her husband slid the contract of sale over to her to sign he was buying her a piece of eternity and that this eternity did not have a single hole in it anywhere.

Even today when she hears someone speak of the war she thinks first of the war that her own body began to wage against her just as the first bombs fell on Germany. Despite the shrinking supplies of food, her body had, utterly illogically, grown fat all at once while others who had been fat beforehand, her sisters for example, first grew slender with all the excitement and then the hunger, and then they grew thin and then haggard. The 6th Army capitulated outside of Stalingrad, and already the morning of that day she was overcome by hot flashes, the sweat covered the space between her lips and nose like a moustache of tiny droplets, this sweat was embarrassing, but it would have embarrassed her even more to wipe it away, the Russians were marching toward Poland, and she felt dizzy, often several times a day, so that she had to steady herself by grasping table edges and door handles so as not to fall down, and finally, just as the Allies were landing in Normandy, even weeping returned to her body, taking hold of it and refusing to leave again, like a long-forgotten creditor come to collect on a debt she no longer recalled. She who had always cut such a boyish figure now stood there every morning before the mirror sweating, she steadied herself on the edge of the sink so as not to fall down, she wiped her tears, avoiding the sight of that round, milky face with which she shared no memories; compared to this face the colored glass in the windows to the right and left of the mirror looked so much more familiar—glass that her husband had put there just because she wanted him to.

She was feeling so poorly during this period that she'd had to ask one of her nieces to come stay with her to help out around the house while her husband was closing down his office in Berlin, packing up the construction plans and organizing a fireproof hiding place for his documents. How good it was that the telephone sat so close beside her bed in its niche, for now she generally kept to her bed even during the day. As she held the receiver to her ear, listening to her husband tell her who had been buried in the rubble, which building had collapsed and how crowded it was down in the cellar, she gazed at the colorful feathers of the little bird that sat forged to her balcony railing, and behind the bird the leafless branches of the trees, and through the branches of the trees the Märkisches Meer glittering. Only after the battle at Seelower Höhen had she sent her niece to stay with relatives in the West to shield her from an encounter with the Slavic hordes, while she herself took refuge behind the double door of the walk-in closet with the last of the provisions and a bit of water. And then the Russian came.

She doesn't want to think that word, that word he called her, that unthinkable word with which he drilled a hole in her eternity for all eternity. Her body, already infertile by then, had drawn him to her—this man who knew the word that robbed her of all strength—had drawn him violently to her and for the length of time a birth might take had smothered the laughter that had stood in her body's way all this time, and during this night in the hidden closet that her husband had built specially for her, because back when she was still a circus princess she had wanted him to, she had finally joined forces with the enemy. Only after the capital had fallen was her husband able to return to her, and what he found was a trampled garden and a gardener weeping at the devastation. His wife shared with him the half loaf of bread the Russian had left for her.

Have you heard this one? A musician is on tour. His very pregnant wife is supposed to let him know when their child is finally born. Their code word is to be: cantaloupe. So the musician is sitting on stage playing. And now one evening a colleague whispers to him from the wings: cantaloupe, cantaloupe, cantaloupe—two with stems, the other, nope! There are things you can't help laughing at every time. This joke is always a success, everyone always laughs, the architect always laughs, and his wife laughs too, even though she's the one who told the joke, and their guests also laugh. Musician on tour, cantaloupe, nope. Around fifteen years ago, the actor Liedtke, who was married to an operetta diva and lived at the end of the sandy road, had done her one better and, using his hands to suggest ample breasts, had quoted from *The Merry Widow*: On account of my melons—um, millions! Musician on tour, cantaloupe, nope; it even worked during the war when the coffee and tea importer from next door told them that the butcher's daughter had just given birth to twins even though her husband hadn't been on furlough from the Eastern front in over a year. Musician on tour, cantaloupe, nope, the architect's wife says today to the director of the State Combine for Automobile Tires, a friend of her husband's, once the laughter has died down: You know, I found it utterly outrageous for Hitler to demand that we women bear children for the state—we aren't machines. And her husband says: In her own way, my wife was practically in the Resistance. The director of the State Combine for Automobile Tires laughs, and the architect laughs, and his wife laughs as well.

All the while, for nearly six years now, time has been draining away through that hole the Russian drilled in her eternity near the end of the war. Only because times are hard has something like a historical moment of inertia set in, only because times are so hard that time has trouble even just running away—it's having to take its time—does the architect's wife still sit there on her terrace six years after the war, sit there with a pot filled with crabs boiled till they are red, serving up her guaranteed punch lines to her friends, laughing herself harder than anyone, and gazing out over the lake that has meanwhile become state property. Time is draining away as the architect's wife, on her husband's arm, accompanies her guests down to the gate and waves after them in the dark, draining away as the couple goes back inside again, as they stack up the plates covered in crab shells and carry them into the kitchen, as she says to him that she's tired already, and he says he wants to smoke one last cigarette outside, as she walks up the stairs, undresses in her room, puts on the silk robe and goes into the bathroom, the colored glass panes in the windows to the right and left of the mirror are even blacker than other glass at nighttime, draining away as the woman sits down on the edge of her bed to rub her legs with camphor oil and her chest with peppermint salve, draining away as she calls out "good night" through the half-open balcony door to her husband, who is smoking one last cigarette down on the terrace, draining away and away as she hangs the cream-colored silk robe back on its hook in the shallow part of the walk-in closet, away and away as she lies down and falls asleep. Away. Soon she will be living in a one-bedroom apartment in West Berlin, and later in a retirement home near Bahnhof Zoo. From her escape to the West until the end of her life, she will always keep everything one might urgently need in an emergency on hand in her purse, things such as paper clips, rubber bands, stamps, scraps of paper to write on and pencils. And in her testament she will leave the property beside the lake and the house that unto all eternity will smell of camphor and peppermint—that house that in purely legalistic terms still belongs to her even though it is located in a country she may no longer set foot in without risking arrest—to her nieces and the wives of her nephews. But not to any man.

THE GARDENER

IN THE SPRING, using a plan sketched out by the householder, an apiary for twelve colonies is set up facing south on the newly acquired land right next to the fruit trees, both to increase the yield of the trees and to provide honey as an additional benefit. Next to the room with the beekeeping equipment is a room for extracting the honey, and since the gardener, who has an excellent grasp of apiculture, will henceforth be spending all his time not devoted to the upkeep of the garden tending the bees, he soon installs a makeshift bed in the extractor room and finally, with the householder's permission, moves in altogether.

The Polish forced laborers in the village say that the potato beetles, which have long since crossed the Oder, are now making their way through Poland. In summer the gardener waters the flowerbed twice a day along with the cypress tree on the side of the house facing the sandy road, and he also waters the roses on the terrace facing the lake, as well as the forsythia bushes, the lilac and the rhododendrons along the edge of the big meadow: once early in the morning, and once at dusk. He begins to make a habit of smoking cigars so the smoke will keep the bees away when he sits on the threshold of the apiary to rest. In fall he rakes up the leaves beneath the big oak tree and burns them, he saws the dry branches from the pine trees, saws them up, splits the pieces and stacks the logs in the woodshed.

THE GIRL

NOW NO ONE KNOWS she is here any longer. All around her everything is black, and the core of this black chamber is she herself. The circumstance that there isn't even a narrow crack to let the light in is intended to save her life, but it also means there is no longer anything differentiating her from the darkness. She would like to have some sort of proof that she is here, but there is no proof. She Doris daughter of Ernst and Elisabeth twelve years old born in Guben. To whom do these words now belong in such darkness? While she sits on the little crate, and her knees bump against the opposite wall, and she moves her legs now to the right, now to the left so they don't fall asleep, time is passing. Probably time is passing. Time that is probably taking her further and further from the girl she perhaps once was: Doris daughter of Ernst and Elisabeth twelve years old born in Guben. No one is there any longer who might be able to tell her whether these words have been abandoned and have only accidentally found their way into this chamber, this head, or whether they truly belong to her. Time has wedged itself between her and her parents, between her and all other people, time has dragged her off and locked her away in this dark chamber. The only thing here that has color is what she remembers in the midst of all this darkness surrounding her, whose core she is, she harbors colorful memories in her light-forsaken head, memories belonging to someone she once was. Probably was. Who was she? Whose head was her head? To whom did her memories now belong? Did black time keep going on and on, even when a person was no longer doing anything but just sitting there, did time keep going on, dragging even a child who has turned to stone away with it?

Gurkenberg and Black Horn, Keperling, Hoffte, Nackliger and Bulzenberg. And Mindach's Hill. When her uncle lifted her up that day to the hump of the pine tree, it seemed to her as if from high up like that she really could recognize all the undersea mountains in the water whose names the gardener had told her and which she still remembered today. Atop the highest elevation stood the church tower of a sunken city, its tip reached so high that the weathervane on top nearly surfaced amid the waves. Down on the bottom where the water was quite calm, on the streets and squares of this city, she could even make out people if she squinted, they were walking about, sitting or standing, leaning up against something or other—through the glittering surface of the lake she saw the silent throng of all those inhabitants of the city who had sunk beneath the waves along with it, who moved about quite naturally in the water without needing to breathe, walking, sitting or standing in this eternal life no differently than they had done before on Earth. She had squatted up there in the pine tree, holding on to its scaly trunk, and from there she saw the fish swimming about in the submerged sky above the city. After her uncle had lifted her down again, her hands were all sticky from the pine resin, and her father had taken sand and used it to rub the resin off.

As the girl sits there in her dark chamber and from time to time tries to straighten up but keeps knocking her head against the ceiling of her hiding place, as she opens her eyes wide but nevertheless cannot even see the walls of her chamber, as the darkness is so great that the girl can't even recognize where her body stops, her head is visited by memories of days on which her entire field of vision was overflowing with colors. Clouds, sky and leaves, the leaves of oak trees, leaves of the willow hanging down like hair, black dirt between her toes, dry pine needles and grass, pine cones, scaly bark, clouds, sky and leaves, sand, dirt, water and the boards of the dock, clouds, sky and gleaming water in which the sun is reflected, shady water beneath the dock, she can see it through the cracks when she lies on her belly on the warm boards to dry off after a swim. After the departure of her uncle, her grandfather continued to take her sailing for another two summers. Surely her grandfather's boat is still in the village shipyard. Four years in winter quarters. Now, without knowing whether it is day or night outside, the girl reaches out to grasp the hand her grandfather is holding out to her, she climbs from the dock onto the edge of the boat and watches her grandfather untie the knot that is holding the boat fast to the dock and toss the rope into the boat.

All the windows of the building on the street called Nowolipie where the girl is hiding are still wide open, until just a few days ago all the rooms were filled with human beings who wanted to breathe, but now everything is completely still. The people from the rooms are gone, and even down below on the street there is no longer anyone walking, no one is pulling a cart, no one is talking, shouting or crying, not even the wind can be heard any longer, no window slams, no door. While the girl sits in her dark chamber and turns her knees now to the right, now to the left, while beyond the chamber everything in the apartment is still, and beyond the apartment everything down in the street is still, and even beyond this street in all the other streets of the district everything is completely still, the girl hears everything that ever was: The rustling of leaves, the splashing of waves, the horn of the steamboat, the dipping of oars into water, the workers next door making a racket, a flapping sail. From C major you retreat by way of G major, D major, A major, E major and B major, going all the way to F-sharp major, further and further one sharp at a time. But from F-sharp back to C is only a tiny step. From playing all the black keys to playing all the white keys is the briefest of journeys, just before you return to the easy-as-pie key of C major everything's swarming with sharps. That's how he explained it to her before he left for South Africa, Uncle Ludwig, and in just this way Doris now, in this complete stillness and emptiness, sets her memory bumping up against the time when everything was still there.

Now only a brief transition still lies before her. Either she will starve to death here in her hiding place, or she will be found and carted off. None of the people who once knew who she was knows any longer that she is here. This is what makes the transition so insignificant. Step by step she has made her way to this place, almost to the end, in other words, her path must have had a beginning, and at the point of this beginning she must have been separated from life by as insignificant a distance as now separates her from death. The beginning must have looked almost exactly like life, it must have been right in the middle somewhere and not yet recognizable as the first part of this path that is leading her somewhere she only now recognizes. When the willow tree has grown up tall and can tickle the fish with its hair, you'll still be coming here to visit your cousins, and you'll remember the day you helped plant it. Was life still intact back then? When she thinks of Uncle Ludwig, she always sees him with the spade in his hand on the shore of the lake. When she thinks of his fiancée Anna, it occurs to her how Anna always told her to make herself light before she picked her up. As if the girl could reduce her weight just by thinking it. When her grandfather gave the towels of his own manufacture a glance before locking up the bathing house but then left the key in the lock for his successor, she had thought of his boat which this summer would remain on dry land for the first time. In the fall her parents sent her to Berlin to stay with an aunt so that she would no longer be subjected to teasing at school because of her Jewish blood. For two years, Sunday after Sunday, always after services at the church at Hohenzollernplatz, she had sat down at the window in her aunt's kitchen and written a letter to her parents, but from Monday to Saturday she didn't write, so as to save envelopes and postage. For the last meal she shared with her grandparents, who were rounded up in Levetzowstrasse in Berlin-Moabit and taken away, her aunt had made stuffed peppers. On New Year's Eve a friend gave her a little bowl filled with cotton and lentils. If you kept the cotton moist, a little forest would sprout from the lentils. During the big wool collection in January she hesitated to hand over not just her caps and the big scarf but also the little scarf because she could tie it up like a turban and then at least her ears would stay warm, but what if someone saw? When their visa for Brazil continued to be delayed, she started going to school wearing thin leather shoes instead of boots in -12° Celsius weather as a precaution, to harden herself for Poland, for in Poland it would surely be even colder than in Berlin. She was to burn her father's last letter, the girl's mother wrote, because of the danger of contagion. The law that would have allowed the girl to travel home by train for her father's funeral did not take effect in time. The lake on which the property lay that had once belonged to her uncle and where she had spent another two summers with her grandparents after her uncle's departure was located exactly in the middle between Berlin and Guben. Was she, Doris daughter of Ernst and Elisabeth twelve years old born in Guben, halfway distant from her life at that point, or more, or less?

Now she has to pee, but she cannot leave the chamber, that's what her mother said before she left for work. Her mother will not come back again, for meanwhile all the occupants of the apartment are gone, all the occupants of the building on the street called Nowolipie, and all the occupants of the district in which the building stands. The district has no doubt been cordoned off meanwhile, for it has been completely still for a very long time now. But as long as this sentence still stands, her name is still Doris, and she still exists: Doris daughter of Ernst and Elisabeth twelve years old born in Guben. So she gets up, knocks her head against the ceiling of her hiding place and tries to pee in such a way that the board on which she has been sitting does not get wet.

Sienna, Pańska and Twarda, Krochmalna, Chłodna, Grzybowska, Ogrodowa, Leszno and Nowolipie, where the girl is hiding, then Karmelicka, Gęsia, Zamenhofa and Miła. When you die at age twelve, do you also reach old age earlier? Everything had kept getting less, they'd had to leave behind more and more baggage, or else it was taken from them, as though they were now too weak to carry all those things that are a part of life, as though someone were trying to force them into old age by relieving them of all this. Two woolen blankets they had— no featherbed—provisions for five days, wristwatch, handbag, no documents. This is how her mother, leading her by the hand, had entered the ghetto, and even the part of the city they had entered had already been relieved of many things. There were no trees there, let alone a park, but there wasn't a river either, there were no automobiles, no electric streetcars and so few remaining streets that it didn't even take the length of a Lord's Prayer to rattle off their names. Everything that was still the world could easily be traversed on foot, even by a child. And this world had gone on shrinking as the end approached. At first the small ghetto was emptied out and dissolved, now it was the turn of the southern part of the large ghetto, and the rest was sure to follow soon thereafter. Don't be so wild, her father had always said to her when she went skidding across the parquet from one end of the room to the other, now she was being a wild child here, but what being wild meant here was: not going instead of some other girl, not offering her head to be counted, playing dead instead of reporting to die, trying to survive without drinking or eating. Never in her life has she been wilder than in this tiny chamber in which she doesn't speak, doesn't sing, can't stand up and, when she sits, keeps banging her knees against the wall. She, Doris daughter of Ernst and Elisabeth twelve years old born in Guben, a wild child, a blind and deaf old woman scarcely capable of moving her limbs any longer.

In Brazil, her father had said, you'll need a hat for the sun. Are there lakes in Brazil too? Of course. Are there trees in Brazil too? Twice as tall as here. And our piano? It won't fit, her father had said and then shut the door of the container, which now held her desk and several suitcases filled with linens and clothes, and her bed with the mattresses and all her books, closed it and locked it. This container was surely still standing on the lot of some shipping company in Guben, but all of this was so long ago that her bed, if she were now to arrive in Brazil, would be much too short for her, and the shirts and stockings and skirts and blouses several sizes too small. Their apartment in Guben had been dissolved when they packed the container for their move to Brazil; after this the girl had been sent to Berlin, and her parents' address to which she sent her Sunday letters changed several times from one shabby part of Guben to an even shabbier one. But as long as there was still hope that they would be allowed to emigrate, it didn't seem important to her parents or her that they'd had to pull the rug out from under their own memories when they packed for the journey to Brazil. When her father received the notice to report for forced labor at the autobahn construction site, the refrigerator built to withstand the heat of the tropics was still standing in the container on the lot of the shipping company. Only after her father's death did it become clear that the packing up of their everyday existence in Guben into this darkness had in truth been an anticipation of their own being packed up, and that both these things were final.

The only place that can still be counted on to resemble itself and of which the girl would be able to say even from here in her dark chamber what it looks like at the present hour is Uncle Ludwig's property. Perhaps that is why she remembers the few weekends and the two summers she spent there more clearly than anything else. On Uncle Ludwig's property she can still walk from tree to tree and hide behind the bushes, she can look at the lake and know that the lake is still there. And as long as she still remembers something in this world, she isn't yet in the foreign place.

And indeed it had already happened weeks before, precisely on that day in June when her mother had gone to Gęsia to sell the wristwatch on the black market and she herself, waiting beside a book stand on Ulica Karmelicka, had discovered the book her mother had refused all that time to let her read, a novel with the title *Saint Gunther or The Man without a Homeland*, on precisely that day when she, standing on Karmelicka, struggling a little to hold her ground amid the press of people, leafed through this book and read and was happy that the owner of this portable booth lacked the strength to prevent her from reading the book without paying for it, precisely on that day all their possessions from their household in Guben were removed from the shipping container in reverse order from the way her father and mother had packed them into this container two years before in preparation for their journey to Brazil, removed by one Herr Carl Pflüger and the chief inspector Pauschel who had been assigned to him, removed and then prepared for auction. On that very day when she spent so long standing there on Karmelicka reading, because she didn't have any money to buy the book and, as long as she kept reading, she didn't have to think about stuffed peppers or pancakes with applesauce or even just a simple slice of bread with butter and salt, precisely on this day in June, approximately two months following her arrival in Warsaw, her childhood bed from Guben, lot number 48, was sold unbeknownst to her for Mk. 20. —to Frau Warnitscheck of Neustädter Strasse 17, her cocoa pot, lot number 119, to Herr Schulz of Alte Poststrasse 42, just a few buildings down from the building in which they'd lived, and her father's concertina, lot number 133, for Mk. 36. —to Herr Moosmann, Salzmarktstrasse 6. On the evening of this day on which she returned to her quarters only just before curfew, on this evening of one of the longest days of the year 1942, on which a faint early-summer breeze was lifting up the newspapers that covered the bodies of the dead and the odor of decay rose into the air, on this evening when it was still light out and she, as she had grown accustomed to doing here, was walking home in zigzags so as not to trip over corpses, on the evening of this day on which, as on all the other evenings, the crying of motherless children rose up in the hallways of the buildings, on this Monday evening on which her mother served her the potatoes she'd gotten in exchange for the wristwatch, very probably the last potatoes she will ever have eaten in her life, already on this evening all the bed sheets belonging to Ernst, Elisabeth and Doris, auctioned off by the pair at prices ranging between 8 marks 40 and 8 marks 70, lot numbers 177 to 185, lay neatly pressed in the linen cupboards of the families Wittger, Schulz, Müller, Seiler, Langmann and Brühl, Klemker, Fröhlich and Wulf.

As dark as it is here, it was probably just as dark under the boat that time when it capsized right near the shore when the boy from the village was trying to sail it up to the dock. Before he walked back to the village, the girl had brought him to the raspberry bushes up by the sandy road. Later the boy had returned the favor by showing her how to swim. Right next to the shore where the water was so shallow that her feet grazed the bottom as she swam, she experienced for the first time the sensation of having the water buoy her up. It was this same summer that the woman from next door had showed her how to catch crabs. But did crabs exist? A lake, a boat, raspberry bushes? Was this boy still there if she couldn't see him? Was there anyone else besides her left in the world? Now something is becoming clear to her that she has failed to consider all this time: If no one knows she exists any longer, who will know there is a world when she is no longer there?

She didn't notice that the floor of the old building where she is hiding isn't quite level, and since it is so dark that she cannot see anything at all, she also cannot see how the little rivulet now meanders out under the door of her hiding place into the abandoned kitchen of an abandoned apartment in abandoned Ulica Nowolipie in Warsaw. By the time the Appropriations Commando under the leadership of a German soldier takes over the apartment, the rivulet has formed a little lake on the kitchen floor.

•

For the last time now she has to walk north up Zamenhofa with the sun at her back. Beside her others are walking whom she doesn't know, all fortunate coincidences have now run out of steam, now all of them are finally going home for good. In the empty streets that the procession crosses block after block lie the shattered tables and beds of those who walked this road before them on the paving stones in the shadow of the buildings. Since the ghetto was never particularly large, the girl knows quite precisely what she is leaving behind. Listing the few streets by name doesn't even take as long as reciting the Lord's Prayer.

Schmeling, they say, once put a tree trunk across his shoulders and walked like that the entire way from his summer cottage in the nearby spa town to the swimming hole in the village. This was to strengthen his arm muscles, the boy from the village had said to her. She'd told him she didn't believe him, and the boy had insisted it was true, saying he'd been there himself when Schmeling arrived. At the swimming hole, Schmeling had tossed the tree trunk off his shoulders as if it were made of paper, he'd stretched his arms and then jumped into the water and swum out so far you couldn't see him any longer. One of the villagers had shouted: For Heaven's sake, our Schmeling is drowning! He'd believed it was true and had implored the villager to swim out after the boxer and save his life. But it had just been a joke all along.

Of the one hundred and twenty people in the boxcar, approximately thirty suffocate during the two-hour trip. As a motherless child, she is considered an inconvenience that might interfere with things running smoothly, and so the moment they arrive she is herded off to the side along with a few old people who cannot walk any longer and the ones who went mad during the trip, she is ushered past a pile of clothing as high as a mountain—like the Nackliger, she can't help thinking and remembers her own smile that she smiled that day when the gardener told her the funny name of that underwater shoal. For two minutes, a pale, partly cloudy sky arches above her just the way it would look down by the lake right before it rained, for two minutes she inhales the scent of the pine trees she knows so well, but she cannot see the pine trees themselves because of the tall fence. Has she really come home? For two minutes she can feel the sand beneath her shoes along with a few pieces of flint and pebbles made of quartz or granite; then she takes off her shoes forever and goes to stand on the board to be shot.

Nothing is nicer than diving with your eyes open. Diving down as far as the shimmering legs of your mother and father who have just come back from swimming and now are wading to shore through the shallow water. Nothing more fun than to tickle them and to hear, muffled by the water, how they shriek because they know it will make their child happy.

For three years the girl took piano lessons, but now, while her dead body slides down into the pit, the word piano is taken back from human beings, now the backflip on the high bar that the girl could perform better than her schoolmates is taken back, along with all the motions a swimmer makes, the gesture of seizing hold of a crab is taken back, as well as all the basic knots to be learned for sailing, all these things are taken back into uninventedness, and finally, last of all, the name of the girl herself is taken back, the name no one will ever again call her by: Doris.

THE GARDENER

IN WINTER THE gardener brings the seasoned logs from earlier years up to the house in the wheelbarrow and kindles fires in the heating stoves for the mistress of the house and her niece.

He prunes the apple and pear trees. In spring he helps the mistress of the house carry down the crates in which she has stowed everything of value, to save it from the Russians. He fetches the oars and oarlocks when she is ready to go out in the boat to sink the crates on the shoal of the Nackliger. When the Russians arrive, they place nearly two hundred horses in the garden, around seventy on the smaller meadow beside the house, and around one hundred and thirty on the larger one to the right of the path that leads down to the lake. The horses scrape at the ground that is just beginning to thaw, transforming it into a morass within a single day, the horses eat everything around them that can possibly serve as food: the fresh leaves and blossoms of the forsythia bush, the young shoots of the fir shrubs and the lilac and hazelnut buds. The Russians confiscate the entire supply of honey. By this time the potato beetle, pursuing a course diametrically opposite to the direction in which the Red Army is marching, has already reached the Soviet Union and is preparing to devastate what potato fields there were spared by the Germans.

THE RED ARMY OFFICER

OVERNIGHT ANOTHER TWELVE horses were brought. Now more than two hundred total are standing in the garden, snorting and pawing the ground. The young Red Army officer walks among them as if walking through a stable whose roof is the moonless sky. The smell of animals closes off the garden against the night better than walls could or a gate. Trees black, bushes black, black the grass trampled beneath hooves, black the bodies of the animals that are so familiar to the youth that he could walk blind from horse to horse to make his way back to the house. He has ordered the others to set out once more to search the surrounding countryside for hidden animals. In the house it stinks of the excretions of his men. The more affluent the homes in which they make their quarters, the more shitting takes place, as if it were necessary to employ this method to restore equilibrium to something off kilter. His men, egging each other on, have shat upon the shiny stone floor, pissed against the painted door and vomited behind the stove. For this reason he has withdrawn to the upstairs of the house, reserving for his own use a small room with a balcony. He himself pees off the balcony and defecates in the garden, but only because he would rather be alone for these activities. Only recently, now that they have penetrated deep into German territory, has the fury of the soldiers reached such a level that they are using the insides of their own bodies to wage war. The more German houses they set foot in, the more painfully they are faced with the question of why the Germans were unable to remain in a place where nothing at all, not the slightest little thing, was lacking.

The young Red Army officer has kept his distance from many things the older soldiers have gotten into, but this does not include battle. This is why he is already a major although his skin still displays the downy radiance of a child. He enlisted voluntarily at the age of fifteen after his mother, father and sisters had all been killed by the Germans. The first one he'd found was his little sister, just four years old, when he returned from the paddock to the family's home. She was floating in the well, face-up. The night before she'd still been lying beside him in the bed they shared, breathing. From then on he had always been right on the front line, and at some point the driving-out had given way to a taking-in, and the defense of his homeland became a ravaging of foreign lands that he would otherwise surely never in his life have set foot in. Like a weed that is ripped from the earth and then thrown through the air in a high arc, he was being carried on by a force that lay outside himself, outside his still youthful body, a force that caused him to march and fight and seize in order to push the Germans further and further across the map, pushing them beyond the borders of their own country, all the way through Switzerland or France or Austria and Italy, further and further until they were shoved into the Mediterranean or the Atlantic, and plunging after them into the depths, sinking further and further to a place where both their movements and his own would be drowned in the same silence. His little sister had probably run out of the house and been caught there by the Germans. His father, his mother and his older sister had burned together with their house. The hands, breasts and eyes of his mother had burned inside the house.

All around the bed in which he now sleeps, the wall is covered to half its height with pink silk. This silk conceals large wooden flaps that are set into the wall and can be opened with a four-sided key, and behind the flaps was the bedding he's been sleeping in for several days now. The bedding smells of peppermint and camphor, as does the cream-colored morning coat he found hanging inside a shallow closet across from the bed. This shallow closet, flanked to the right and left by wooden columns, is set into the wall like a door and opens with a brass knob. On the inside of the door of this closet a full-length mirror is mounted. When he moved into the room, the young Red Army officer had opened the door to see what was behind it, he'd seen the morning coat hanging there and, without knowing why, he'd taken the cloth in his hands and inhaled its fragrance, peppermint and camphor, and meanwhile the mirror had mutely reflected his image from his short Russian hair to the now very thin soles of his boots in which he had marched all the way from his homeland to here, all this reflected in the German mirror, and then the youth had closed the door again. Sometimes when he is alone in the room in the evening he goes over to the shallow closet, opens it without knowing why, buries his face for a little while in the cream-colored fabric, ignoring his mirror image, then at some point closes the door again and goes to bed. Tonight, too, he puts his hands into the smooth, lustrous cloth, pulls it to his face, rubs it between his fingers, rubs the fabric's rough inner surface against its rough inner surface, fills his lungs with the scent of peppermint and camphor before he closes the door and lies down on the bed, all around him the walls covered in pink silk; the balcony door is open to the darkness, and down in the garden the horses are softly neighing and pawing the earth and snorting in the huge muffled stall that extends all the way to the stars.

And then there is one additional sound this night, a rustling sound like the sound of the martens that make their nests in the attic, he'd caught one of them yesterday, and the creature's fur is now hanging over the railing of the little balcony, once more a rustling comes from behind the wall in which the shallow closet is set. The young Red Army officer gets up quickly, before there's even time for him to think that if things are as they should be, there's no room for a marten inside a wall. He opens the door, and at once everything falls silent behind the wall on which the morning coat is hanging. Only now does he step back and examine the shallow closet from top to bottom, he examines the wooden columns that flank it, and only now does he see that they don't quite reach all the way to the floor, in the few millimeters left between the columns and the floor, he sees, kneeling down on the floor now, the outermost curve of tiny wheels almost entirely concealed in the interior of the columns. Only now does he see that the soft cork floor directly in front of the shallow closet has been polished in a half-circle, even though the door with the mirror on it always opened easily. In the remaining fractions of a second in which he thinks and grasps all these things, he also thinks and grasps that on the other side of the shallow cupboard someone is breathing who already knows all his thoughts and is now awaiting the end of this very, very long second.

He reaches for his revolver, quietly closes the mirrored door, and then gives a strong quick tug on the metal knob without turning it first. As expected, one of the wooden columns now emerges from the paneling of the wall, and with a faint squeaking sound the shallow closet follows his energetic tug as if the youth had just opened the thick page of a wooden book. He peers into a deep closet that had previously been hidden, he sees jackets, dresses, coats, shirts and blouses hanging close together one beside the other, and in a compartment above them sweaters, scarves and hats. The closet's rod and shelf extend off into the darkness to the right of the door. And there something is rustling, but the young Red Army officer cannot see. A vibrant odor—urine and feces—engulfs him, and beneath the hanging clothes he sees a pot filled to the brim with filth. Some defecate out of fear, others because they cannot come out of their hiding places, and still others out of anger, he thinks, and all of this together is called war. Maybe the Germans used to hide too much, it occurs to him, now that he has happened upon this secret closet, they even hid the bedclothes in the wall and put up wooden gratings to hide the radiators. And they weren't even taking into account that the war might come washing back over them, they concealed all these things from their own eyes alone. Now finally everything is being dragged back out again: clothes, jewelry, bicycles, livestock, horses and women. Now everyone else sees it, and they themselves are being forced to see it as well. Everything is being dragged out into the light and put to use, anyone still alive stops washing himself, and anyone buried beneath the rubble rots and thus also begins to stink.

The Red Army officer forces his way between the clothes, his revolver pointed into darkness, to the back of the closet where he encounters a body that mutely begins to put up resistance when he reaches for it. Before the war, the Red Army officer was still a child, and making use of women had never interested him during the war, but here, as he puts his revolver away so as to be able to use both hands to hold fast what is struggling here in his grasp, he is so occupied with seizing and grasping and forced by this seizing and grasping into such close proximity that before he can even consider what he is doing, he touches the warm breasts of a woman in the dark, a woman who is continuing to struggle and in this struggle forcing him to ever greater proximity, then he feels her hair on his face and finally, when he has forced her into the farthest corner and she bites his arm and he twists both her arms behind her back, he catches a whiff of camphor and peppermint, this smell of illnesses one waits out lying in bed, this smell of maturity and peacetime.

Then he grows calm, and calmly he begins to kiss the lips he cannot see, he who has never before kissed anyone on the mouth, he kisses this most probably German mouth that is full and perhaps also slightly wilted, but he cannot judge this because he has never before kissed anyone on the mouth, then he releases her arms and strokes the woman's head, she is no longer struggling, but he hears her begin to cry, he strokes her head as if to comfort her, and then doesn't know what to do next, although he's seen often enough what his men do in comparable situations. *Mama*, he says, without knowing what he is saying, it's so dark that you cannot even see your own words, and she thrusts him away from her, he stumbles, falls down, she kicks him, he tries to grasp her once more and in the process takes hold of her knees, and then she stands still, then she slowly pulls her dress up a little, he rests his forehead against her belly, she appears to be naked under her dress, he inhales the smell of life emanating from the curly hair. She says one or two words, but her words too are invisible in this dark hiding place. Perhaps the war consists only in the blurring of the fronts, for now, as she pushes the soldier's head between her legs, pushing it between her legs perhaps only for the reason that she knows he has a weapon and that it is better not to struggle, she begins to guide him, perhaps war consists only in one person's guiding another out of fear, and then the other way around, and on and on in this way. And as now the young soldier, perhaps only out of fear of the woman, pushes his tongue in among the curly hair, tasting something that tastes like iron, a warm stream begins to flow over his face, first gently, then more forcefully, the woman is urinating on his face, urinating on him in just the way his men urinated on the painted door in the entryway below, and so she too is waging war, or is this love, the soldier doesn't know, the two seem to resemble one another, and now, when it ought to be his turn to take over, to guide her, he remains kneeling there, and amid all the wetness tears have begun to flow down his face, and his tears have the same temperature as the great river that is flooding him, with which his tears now intermingle here in the depths of a German closet. Instead of taking over, he remains kneeling there at the feet of the woman, sobbing audibly now, but perhaps it is precisely his weakness that disarms the woman far more effectively than force would have done. For now she draws him at last to his feet, dries his face on one of the pieces of clothing between which they are standing, and speaks softly to him. It wouldn't take much for her to push him out of the closet with a little spank, like a mother sending her young son off to school.

Back where he was at home there was no such thing. It's as if his childhood had stopped where his homeland did. Back where his home was, the girls wore two braids on their way to school or else tied these braids into loops with big, red silk ribbons and a triangular neck scarf. When they walked, they held their heads up in a way he has not seen any woman do here in Germany, as if everything that might have weighed them down had been lifted from their shoulders. On summer evenings they went strolling along with their heads held high like this, strolling one last time out to the edge of the field, linking their arms in pairs or even three at a time, chatting and laughing when they saw the boys leaning up against the linden tree, they laughed and went walking past, and the swallows were flying, and the boys were sitting and standing around the linden tree, and sometimes, very rarely, they succeeded in engaging the girls in conversation on their way home, and only one single time did one of the girls take up the boys' offer and sit down on the bench under the linden tree, the boys had all gotten up at once, gangly and downy, and had nudged and shoved one another while the girl remained sitting there for approximately five minutes exchanging wisecracks with them. In his homeland he had never seen women offering themselves openly on the street or in their apartments like here in Germany, nor had he seen indecent pictures or magazines. In a German photography studio two or three towns back, its display windows shattered and its walls falling in, a creased picture had caught his eye while his men were plundering the shop, this picture lay on the floor and in it he had seen a naked woman threatening another naked woman with a whip. This photograph was as far removed from the mosaics adorning the town hall in the larger town near where he grew up as Russia was from Germany. These mosaics had shown women with sheaves of grain in their arms, young students holding test tubes in their hands, and mothers with babies on their hips. To watch a girl undo her braid while bathing and then see her hair tumble down about her shoulders would have been enough, back home, to fall in love, but these women with whips in their hands he associated with the photo studio itself that had been bombed into rubble and then plundered, as though these women were standing upon layer after layer of things that had been trampled, torn up and worn down, and were whipping one another to set everything ablaze with this last malicious pleasure. His men had taken this picture and many other ones like it and were now carrying them around in their uniform jackets, face to face with the photographs of their wives and children. In school he had learned that the seed for the happy future of mankind was being sowed in the Soviet Union. But now, on his journey through Germany, this journey that was the war, an unsavory dirty past that until then had been unknown to these Soviet men was catching up with them and dragging them deeper in this foreign land. And yet, if you stopped to consider that since the beginning of the war Poland had all but ceased to exist, there was now a border where Russia and Germany met.

Amid all this silence the woman goes on the attack again, she attacks him right in the middle—stop dreaming all the time, his mother always said to him—she seizes his cock right through his trousers and pushes the youth to the ground, she's much stronger than he is, and now she throws herself on top of him, there's nowhere to take cover here, she wants to cover him, this mare, with experienced hands she tears open his trousers and spears herself on him, riding him deeper, then she grabs him in a chokehold and squeezes his throat, whispering curses, he has stopped resisting—if that's what she wants—he drives his barb into her flesh, she holds his mouth shut and spits on his face, she rubs herself against him, he thrusts, she tears open her blouse and slaps her breasts in his face, and he—hears himself moaning, hears himself saying *No* in Russian, and she says *Yes*, so he keeps thrusting, thrusts the mare in two, victory grinding itself against defeat, defeat against victory, and sweat and juices between the peoples, and spurting, spurting until all life has been spurted out, the final cry the same in all languages. Now death has finally been brought to its knees, youth and age as well, no point at all thinking of what was and what will be, now there is nothing left any more, nothing at all, nothing, nothing, just weary breath still drifting between mouths, a leftover scrap of something, limp as the summer dresses hanging beside the heads of the Red Army officer and this woman, who cannot be recognized in the darkness. Last summer, when perhaps she or some other woman wore these dresses, the war had not yet disturbed the peace here.

In fact all he did was open a closet.

Now he shuts the closet door again.

Outside his men are at work, they're just back from their foray. He hears them shouting out in the garden with the horses, shouting and talking, then the shouting and talking enter the house, they call upstairs to him, he says: I'm coming. He goes downstairs, sees his men sprawling on the long bench seat, herrings are lying on grease-soaked paper on the long table, bread as well, someone else is just adding a bottle of vodka. No more horses, they say, all we found were a few German uniforms in the woods, not hidden very well, under leaves. They say: The Germans have flown the coop. One of them is just trying on one of the German coats. Not bad, he says, it fits. On the floor lies his Soviet coat, badly tattered. That's a good idea, another one says and begins to undress. I'm going to sleep down here tonight, the young major says. Guess you were scared all by yourself, says one of the older soldiers with a laugh and shouts: Go on, give him the cushions from the bench; two others remove a cushion hanging from little brass hooks, hooting once the wall behind it comes into view: It is covered with leather. There's my new boots, shouts one of the two and pulls out a knife. Not so fast, says the young major, the boots are for me. He pushes the table to one side, takes the cushion and tosses it to the man wearing the German coat, grabs the knife from the hand of the other one, who says: The little man always gets screwed, grinning, because he is much larger and stronger than the major and everyone can see this, and now the others grin too as he kneels down on the bench to be able to cut better. There are two remaining cushions, he removes both of them and tosses them to the others, square after square he cuts out the leather, twelve powerful strokes, he cuts decisively but not at all greedily, as though this were merely some necessary operation he was performing to save a wounded man. Two men meanwhile begin to fight over the remaining German coat. Another belches. One lies down on the bench beside the stove to go to sleep and says: Just like home. Outside it is growing light already, but the colored bull's eye panes in the windows make dawn in this house green. Two hours of sleep, then the horses must be gotten ready, and we leave again at noon, the major says. He stacks the squares of leather one atop the other, rolls them up and places them, as he now lies down on the cushions to go to sleep, as a leather roll beneath his head.

In the morning, when the others are already busy driving the horses out of the garden onto the sandy road, he takes half a loaf of bread and goes back up to the bedroom one last time. There he plucks the marten pelt from the railing of the balcony, throws it over his shoulder, then goes over to the closet, grabs hold of one of the fake columns and yanks open the door. Without looking inside, he throws the heel of the bread back into the darkness, then closes the door and leaves the room. With the pelt dangling over his shoulder, an uncured skin, and the roll of leather in his coat pocket, he looks like a hunter. At home, in his village, there was one like that, he had gotten so used to living in the woods that he returned to human society only to sell or trade his kill for weapons and ammunition. He felt more at home among the animals who sooner or later became his quarry than among human beings. Sometimes he stayed away from the village for a long time, and then he'd start coming again, so that you couldn't tell whether or not he'd died yet. Now it seemed the village no longer existed, but perhaps the hunter was still roaming through the woods. Or else he'd long since lain down among the animals and died there, finally his own quarry.

THE GARDENER

AFTER THE RUSSIANS have pulled out, the gardener prunes
the shrubs and bushes in the hope that they might bud a second time. He turns the soil of the big and small meadows and
sets out potatoes forty centimeters apart. The potato plants require a lot of water. The gardener fetches the oars and oarlocks
from the workshop for the mistress of the house and assists her
in retrieving the crates sunk on the shoal of the Nackliger and
bringing them back to the house. He extracts the honey. In the
evening he sits on the threshold of the apiary and smokes a cigar, at nightfall he lies down to sleep on his cot beside the drum
of the extractor. When the potatoes have reached a height of fifteen to twenty centimeters, he hills the plants. He gives the dock
a coat of pine tar and replaces the rotten boards. He prunes the
willow tree beside the shore whose twigs have grown down so
low over the edge of the dock that they get in your way when
you step out onto it. He places new frames in the beehives. He
pulls out the weeds growing between the roses and in the flowerbed in front of the house. He waters the shrubs, potatoes and
flowers twice a day, once early in the morning and once at dusk.
When the foliage of the potato plants begins to wither, it is time
for the harvest, and he stores the potatoes in the cool, dark cellar. In fall he rakes up the leaves, burns them, covers the rose-
bed and the flowerbed before the house with spruce twigs to

protect the plants from the frost, when fall is coming to an end he empties all the water pipes in the house and turns off the main spigot, he closes all the shutters including those of the bathing house down by the water. He retrieves the electric heating coil from the cellar and sets it up near his bed in the extractor room. In winter he prunes the apple and pear trees. He heats the house in advance when the architect and his wife are planning a visit and turns the water back on for the length of their stay.

In spring he helps the householder erect a fence in front of the house to enclose the flowerbed with its cypress tree, the entrance to the garage and above all the big gate, to protect the house from unwanted visitors. The gardener prunes the shrubs, re-plants grass on the two potato fields, helps empty the cesspit, he pulls out weeds, waters the bare dirt of the big and small mead-ows until the grass begins to sprout, he harvests cherries, har-vests apples and pears, stores them in the cellar of the house, rakes the leaves, burns them, saws off dry branches, splits the wood, retrieves the heating coil from the cellar and sets it up near his bed in the extractor room, during the winter he sets traps in the attic for the martens. He heats the house in advance when the architect and his wife are planning a visit. In spring, he prunes the apple and pear trees, he uncovers the beds, prunes the shrubs, pulls up weeds, swaps out the frames in the beehives; in summer, he runs the sprinkler twice a day and prunes the cherry trees. In fall he chops wood and smokes out the moles, at the beginning of winter he empties all the water pipes in the house.

When several years later the blue spruce is blown over just be-fore New Year's, it barely misses the thatched roof of the house. It falls right across the path that leads between the small and big meadows down to the water, and is heavy enough to crush several rosebushes in the bed beside the terrace. The gardener saws up the trunk, splits the pieces and stacks the logs down in the woodshed. In spring when he is digging up the rose-bed to replace the dead plants with new ones, he discovers a chest filled with silver. Since the house is sealed, he takes the chest for safekeeping and places it, just as it is, on a shelf in the extractor room next to the jars of honey.

The following year, the municipality issues the gardener a permit to continue to make his residence in the extractor room and entrusts him with the keys to workshop and woodshed. For a spring, a summer, a fall and a winter the gardener continues to tend the now ownerless garden just as before: He fertilizes, waters, prunes, swaps out the frames in the beehives, extracts the honey, wraps the trunks of the fruit trees with cloth to keep the deer that leap over the fence from chewing the bark; the gardener weeds, harvests, rakes, burns, saws, splits, smokes out and covers beds with spruce twigs. What he needs to live he acquires from the farmers by bartering fruit, firewood and honey. A year and a quarter later, new householders arrive, having leased the property from the municipality: A writer couple from Berlin. The gardener shows them the garden, the workshop, the woodshed, the dock and the bathing house, as well as the apiary for twelve colonies and the extractor room and gives them the keys.

The new householder seeks out the gardener to discuss several changes with respect to the garden. A staghorn sumac is to be placed at the center of the small meadow, and at the center of the large one a maple. The gardener digs the holes for the plants. After working his way through the thin layer of humus, he first strikes bedrock that has to be broken up with his spade, and only beneath this is the layer of sand with the groundwater coursing through it, and finally beneath the sand the blue clay found everywhere in this region. The gardener excavates the holes up to a depth of eighty centimeters and fills the bottom with composted soil so the staghorn sumac and the maple will flourish.

•

After consultation with the householder, the gardener fills the hollow in the trunk of the walnut tree with concrete to give the tree greater stability. He fertilizes the flowers, the shrubs and the freshly planted trees, mows the grass of the two meadows, swaps out the frames in the beehives, extracts the honey, he harvests cherries, twice a day in summer he waters the rose-bed and the flowerbed next to the house and the shrubs; meanwhile he turns on the sprinkler on the small and big meadows for half an hour daily as well as beneath the fruit trees so that everything will be well irrigated, he prunes the cherries, harvests apples and pears. On instructions from the mistress of the house, he delivers two thirds of both the honey and the harvested fruit to the local FVP, the government trade organization "Fruit, Vegetables and Potatoes."

Together with the new householder, he paves the area in front of the workshop with flagstones to have a better work surface for painting and repairs. In winter, the rowboat along with the iron trestles and the wooden planks for the dock are to be stored there. At the householder's request, the gardener tears down the wooden boat shelter beside the dock—its posts were rotting. The gardener makes urgently needed repairs on the thatch roofs of both the main house and bathing house. In fall he saws up the branches felled by storms from the big oak tree and several of the pines, splits the pieces and stacks the logs in the woodshed, when fall is coming to an end he retrieves the heating coil from the cellar of the house and sets it up beside his bed in the extractor room, and finally at the beginning of winter he empties all the water pipes in the house and turns off the main valve.

The following spring, on instructions from the householder, all the windows of the main house, the bathing house and the extractor room are given a fresh coat of paint, the gardener stuffs more oakum into the gaps between the boards of the bathing house where the walls have become leaky and applies pine tar to renew the waterproofing. Sometimes when he is sitting on the steps of the apiary, smoking a cigar to protect himself from the swarms, the son of the writer couple—who comes only occasionally during vacations for a few days and the rest of the time lives in a home for children—sits down beside him and asks him questions about the life of the bees.

THE WRITER

I A-M G-O-I-N-G H-O-M-E, was the sentence she last wrote on her typewriter yesterday. Now she takes out the sheet of paper and sets it off to the side, sets it on the stack, still not very high, of the already written pages of her new book, she removes a sheet of laid paper with a watermark from a drawer and begins her letter to the general concerning the new neighbor's entitlement to lake access and concerning also the bathing house situated on precisely the bit of shoreline that is at issue—state property that she has been leasing for twenty years now along with the house—she addresses the general by his childhood nickname and in a familiar tone, and while she is writing her fury seeps away and turns into exhaustion. She asks herself what forces are at work here, what might be empowering a local official to speak to her of directives "from higher up." Beneath the shroud of secrecy that a handful of comrades who became accustomed to this shroud during the era of illegality have managed to preserve even now, in this time of reinvented peace, something new is afoot, something even she is unable to recognize.

From her desk she can see the lake shimmering between the reddish trunks of the pine trees. Down in the kitchen the cook is making the plates clatter, the gardener is sitting on the threshold to his room smoking a cigar, on the big meadow her grand-daughter and the boy next door are spraying each other with water, her daughter-in-law is just making her way down to the dock to sunbathe, the visitor is lying in a lawn chair beneath the hawthorn tree, her son is mowing the grass, and down below, in front of the workshop, her husband is painting the fishing stools, whose red paint is flaking off, green. The window stands open, and so she smells the lake and the sunshine, smells the smoke from the gardener's cigar, but also the odor of roast meat rising from the kitchen, she smells the mowed grass and, when the wind turns and begins to blow from below, even the fresh green paint. The tapping of her typewriter mixes with the calls of the cuckoo, letter for letter it can be heard from both upper meadows, all the way down to the workshop and even on the dock, when the wind blows from above to below.

The doctor from the government hospital in Berlin, for whom she had successfully petitioned the municipality to get him permission to lease the orchard and the apiary, immediately had all the fruit trees chopped down—certainly not what they'd agreed on—and then tore down the apiary as well. With supernatural speed, practically overnight, unknown workers from Berlin soon thereafter put up a large house where the apiary had stood, and rumor had it that he'd even been permitted to purchase this house, which went against the usual practice. When she lodged a complaint with the municipality, she was informed that everything had been decided "higher up" and that further instructions had meanwhile been received to grant him lake access by reducing the size of the property she was leasing, the arrangement for a new fence leading down to the water was to be worked out as soon as possible. This young doctor, who hadn't even been born yet when she returned to Germany after years of exile, was meanwhile personal physician to some high-up official and now, it seemed, actually had the gall to make his move against her using the invisible army whose generals she had rocked in her arms during her emigration.

•

She puts the letter in an envelope, addresses and seals it, then she takes up the sheet of paper she'd set aside earlier that morning and puts it back in the typewriter to go on working where she stopped the day before. I a-m g-o-i-n-g h-o-m-e. The keys of the typewriter she writes on have already been rubbed smooth, the individual letters can scarcely be distinguished from one another. It is still the same typewriter she brought with her on that odyssey from Berlin to Prague, from Prague to Moscow, and then from Moscow to Ufa in Bashkiria, and near the end of the war, when her son could already speak Russian fluently, back again to Moscow and finally, Berlin. She carried this typewriter in her hand through many streets of many cities, held it on her lap in overcrowded trains, gripping its handle tightly when in this or that foreign place, alone on an airfield or at a train station, she didn't know where to go, when she'd lost her husband in the throng, or else his duties took him elsewhere and he'd boarded a different train. This typewriter was her wall when the corner of a blanket on a floor was her home, with this typewriter she had typed all the words that were to transform the German barbarians back into human beings and her homeland back into a homeland.

Home, all he wanted was to go home, the German official who'd been installed as mayor in a tiny little town in the so-called Reichsgau Wartheland wrote in his diary after a colleague had reported to him that while he was on vacation all the Jews from the entire region had been rounded up in the church, held there for three days and then loaded into gassing trucks and transported to the woods. The corpses of the ones who had already died during the three days in the church had been tossed into the gas trucks along with the living, the dead children hurled at the heads of their still living parents. Home, all he wanted was to go home, the mayor had written then in his diary. This diary was later included in the materials placed at her disposal for use in her radio show in the Ural region.

By then the impending defeat of the Germans was already becoming quite clear, and every one of the Red Army's victories brought her, her husband and their son who had been born in the Soviet Union that much closer to going back to Germany.

Holding the mayor's diary in her hands, she'd felt disgusted that, as became clear from the further course of the diary, the German official did decide to remain in his post and office after all, that he continued to preside over this small town until the Red Army marched in and he fled to the West. But all the same she could never forget his sentence about just wanting to go home. Home! he'd cried out like a child that would give anything not to be seeing what it was seeing, but precisely in this one brief moment in which he hid his face in his hands, as it were, even this dutiful German official had known that home would never again be called Bavaria, the Baltic coast or Berlin, home had been transformed into a time that now lay behind him, Germany had been irrevocably transformed into something disembodied, a lost spirit that neither knew nor was forced to imagine all these horrific things. H-o-m-e. *Which thou must leave ere long.* After he had swum his way through a brief bout of despair, the German official had applied to retain his post. Those others, though, the ones who had fled their homeland before they themselves could be transformed into monsters, were thrust into homelessness by the news that reached them from back home, not just for the years of their emigration but also, as seems clear to her now, for all eternity, regardless of whether or not they returned. I just want to go home, just home, she'd often thought in those days, and from the Urals had directed her machine gun fire at her homeland, word after word. But now that no one country was to be her homeland any longer but rather mankind in general, doubt continued to manifest itself in her as homesickness.

This morning she and her husband took the long walk up to the forest, to the bench in whose wood her son had already carved his parents' initials with his pocket knife years before. The four letters have long since turned gray. They always stop to rest upon this bench for a while before turning around. They sit and gaze, their eyes following the course of the hill that descends gently to the lake, they watch as the wind stirs the grain field, and behind it they see the broad surface of the lake, leaden, from a distance they cannot see how this same wind is rippling the water, nor do they see the house between the hill and the lake, from this perspective it is hidden in the shadow of the Schäferberg. They look at the ground, close by, at their feet, where yesterday's rain has pressed the sand into little rivulets, they see flint and pebbles of quartz or granite, then they get up again, she takes her husband's arm and the two of them make their way downhill, back to the house, where today he intends to give the fishing stools, whose red paint is flaking off, a coat of green paint, while up in her study she will sit at her desk and write down what she remembers of her life.

This doctor wasn't even born yet when she returned to Germany. He has traveled to Japan with one or the other government delegation, to Egypt, to Cuba. I a-m g-o-i-n-g h-o-m-e. Down in the kitchen the cook is making the plates clatter, the gardener is sitting on the threshold to his room, on the meadow her granddaughter and the boy next door are spraying each other with water, her daughter-in-law is sunbathing on the dock, the visitor is lying in a lawn chair, her son is mowing the grass, her husband is painting the fishing stools green. There are things she remembers but does not write. She doesn't write that she said no when, after Hitler's attack on the Soviet Union a German comrade whose husband had just been arrested came to her with her small child asking to be hidden. No, because her own residence permit had already expired and even she herself could only enter or leave her Moscow quarters at times when no one would see her. She doesn't write that the manuscript for her radio show about the daily work of the German official was corrected by the Soviet comrades. The episode with the Jews in it was cut. That wouldn't appeal to German soldiers, she'd been told, it might possibly hurt the cause and in any case was irrelevant in this context. She who had emigrated not because of her Jewish mother but as a communist had, without putting up a fight, cut that part of her report. She doesn't write that eventually she did begin after all, after several comrades known to be Jews had vanished, to dye her coppery hair that even during her German childhood had caused her to be taunted as a Jew. She doesn't write about how she and her husband were asked by her Soviet comrades to board a train to Novosibirsk. That they hid instead of getting on the train. A German painter from their circle of friends had obeyed the Party's order and boarded a similar train, and then he had starved to death building a dam in Kazakhstan. While outside the cuckoo is calling, her fingers rest upon the typewriter keys.

The poet who hid her back then had written a poem in which he described going home as crossing over to the shores of Death. She had learned to remain silent then, and after all the deprivations, this silence was the greatest gift that had ever been given to their dream, which remained so large that every single one of the comrades was utterly alone when he walked about in it.

The poet who hid her back then now lives with his wife in a summer cottage on the other side of the lake, and this afternoon they will perhaps land at the dock in their motorboat made of dark shiny wood, and then her friend will toss the rope to her husband, her husband will catch the rope and tie it to the dock, and the granddaughter will watch her grandfather and take note of the figure eight the rope makes when it is wound around the cleat.

I a-m g-o-i-n-g h-o-m-e. The actor who built a bungalow a few properties down recently stayed behind in the West after a performance there and will soon be having his wife and son join him. The bungalow has already been sealed. He had wanted light blue tiles for his bathroom. Light blue tiles did not exist in this part of Germany. Where the new person is to begin, he can only grow out of the old one. Cuckoo. Cuckoo. The new world is to devour the old one, the old one puts up a fight, and now new and old are living side by side in a single body. Where much is asked, more is left out.

When they returned to Germany, it was a long time before she and her husband could bring themselves to shake hands with people they didn't know. They had felt a virtually physical revulsion when faced with all these people who had willingly remained behind. After his return, her husband had even hesitated to visit his mother and sisters, who lived in the Western part of Germany. The only visit they ever made to this West German city was undertaken with the sole purpose of showing their son his grandmother, and neither she nor her husband shook hands with his mother or sisters when they greeted them. They saw, too, that this omission occurred by mutual consent. Immediately before they fled to Prague, they had deposited a picture and a few pieces of furniture with her husband's sisters. Her husband's mother and sisters were now sitting at this table, on these chairs, and the picture hung on the wall. And she and her husband now sat on these chairs as if they had come to their own house for a visit. The two Communists were at a loss for the words they would have needed to demand their own possessions back from these Germans to whom they had once been related. Later, when their son was old enough to travel by train without them, they let him make the trip twice on his own when he expressed the desire to visit his grandmother.

Now the gong is calling her to lunch. She walks through the closet room and the hallway to the bathroom, where she washes her hands, her fingertips are smudged with black from changing the ribbon, she looks into the mirror, arranges her hair, closes the right-hand wing of the small window that had been open for air, now the mosaic of colorful squares is complete again.

Before she goes down to eat, she quickly steps back into the Little Bird Room to get a jacket from the wall closet, since it's always chillier than you'd expect inside the house, even in summer. The Little Bird Room got its name from the small iron bird forged to the railing of the balcony. During school holidays, her granddaughter sleeps here. The granddaughter now strikes the gong downstairs for a second time, possibly out of impatience, or else because it's fun.

Even at midday, what strikes the long table through the colorfully glazed windows is more penumbra than light, and around this table sit her husband, their son with his wife and her granddaughter, and often also friends and colleagues from Berlin, comrades or, as today, the visitor, then the cook and finally the gardener. After the soup is brought out, her husband speaks about this and that, her son about something else, her daughter-in-law contributes a remark, the visitor remains silent, the gardener remains silent, the cook serves the main course, she herself elaborates, her daughter-in-law has yet another question, her son says: I don't see how that's possible, her husband says: But it is. She herself says: That's certainly interesting, and: Do take some more potatoes, the visitor says: No thank you, the gardener remains silent, her granddaughter shakes her head, her son says: Send them over, the daughter-in-law: That was delicious, she herself says: It truly was, the gardener says: Thank you, the cook: The soup was a bit too salty, her son says: Not at all, the cook stacks up the dirty plates and balances them out into the kitchen, she returns with tiny little bowls on a tray, distribution of the compote, everyone gets busy with their spoons, general quiet reigns, the door handle is depressed from the outside, giving off a metallic sigh, the boy next door wants her granddaughter to come out and play, he remains standing beside the stove, waiting until everyone has finished eating, the visitor brings her compote cup to her lips and sips the last dregs of juice, her daughter-in-law says to the little girl: But first help clear the table, her husband says: Well, then, she herself nods to the cook. They all get up and leave the room in one direction or other.

I a-m g-o-i-n-g h-o-m-e. No, she and her husband did not *go home* to Germany; what they wanted was to bring this country—only coincidentally the one whose language they spoke—back home again in their thoughts. They wanted finally to drag from beneath the German rubble some ground they could keep beneath their feet, ground that would no longer be illusory. Although their bodies would grow old, their hope for mankind's salvation from greed and envy would, they thought, remain young for a long time, the errors of mortals were mortal, but their work was immortal. And now it is precisely that young doctor whom they allow to examine their aging bodies once a year, that doctor who is taking advantage of the State to become the heir to its founders. It has once more come to pass that the invisible army, now divided, is soundlessly striking its own forces with invisible lances and shields. Perhaps these young people, who know the enemy only from the reports of their elders and have never seen him face to face, will soon be ready to defect and join the ranks of this foe, even if only to have at last the opportunity—after so many years of siege—to take up arms once more.

Have the words in her aging mouth aged as well without her noticing? After supper, the chairs from the garden are set up in the hall so that everyone can join in watching the news on television: she and her husband, their son, their daughter-in-law, her son's little girl, the visitor, some friends or other who will be spending the night in the bathing house, and sometimes the cook as well. On the seven o'clock news they hear about bringing in the harvest, farmers are standing in the dust between rows of stubble talking about planned production targets, combine harvesters can be seen and also silos. Foreign words that did not grow in the farmers' mouths are relegating them to the dust of the fields where they must serve as a focal point. Since her return to Germany, all her passion has been devoted to attempting to use the words she's typed out letter by letter to transform her memories into the memories of others, to transport her life on paper into other lives as if ferrying it across a river. These letters she's been tapping out have allowed her to draw to the surface many things that seemed worthy of preserving, while pushing other things, painful ones, back into obscurity. Now, later, she no longer knows whether it wasn't a mistake to pick and choose, since this thing she'd been envisioning all her life was supposed to be a whole world, not a half one.

Yes, she reads several days later in a statement sent to her from the municipal offices, she too is welcome to purchase her house, but not the land on which it is standing, and the bathing house can, if she so desires, be relocated to the meadow at the top of the hill at government expense, as a way of facilitating the doctor's lake access while at the same time fulfilling the State's obligations to her. She removes from her typewriter the sheet of paper containing certain words and not containing certain other words, sets it on the not particularly high stack of already written pages of her new book, removes a sheet of laid paper from the drawer, rolls it into the machine and responds to the municipal offices: Yes, she would like to purchase her house and of course would be grateful to have the bathing house relocated to the top of the hill. With Socialist greetings.

THE GARDENER

NOW THAT THE WALNUT tree whose hollow was filled with concrete continues to stand upright but has stopped bearing nuts over the past three years, the gardener chops it down at the householder's bidding. He saws up the trunk, splits the pieces and stacks the logs in the woodshed. During the cherry harvest the gardener falls off the ladder and breaks his leg. For two months he has to lie in bed until his bones have knitted together and he can start learning to walk again. Fortunately the son of the householder has begun this summer to spend his entire vacation time on the property, he has been discharged from the Home and is now living with his parents again—and he has meanwhile grown tall and is strong enough to take over the task of mowing the lawn. But the fungus that attacks every last one of the fruit trees this summer goes unnoticed too long during the gardener's convalescence, and so when the gardener gets up again for the first time he finds all the apples and pears withered on their stems.

After his fall, the gardener is no longer able to perform heavy labor. All he's been able to do since then is walk slowly across the property, here and there picking up bits of fallen wood, he trims the dry blossoms from flowers and shrubs, waters shrubs and flowers twice a day, once early in the morning and again when dusk arrives, at the beginning of winter he empties all the water pipes in the house and turns off the main valve. He closes all the shutters, both in the main house and the bathing house down by the lake.

The householder and his son now take over the yearly task of repairing and dismantling the dock. To supplement the heating stove in the house a night storage heater is installed, now the firewood cut in earlier years will readily suffice for charging the stove on chilly spring and autumn days. Apple and pear trees fail to recover from the fungal infestation, even over the next several years. Spider mites attack the cherries. When the garbage pit is expanded, it furthermore becomes clear that the pipes that provide water to the orchard rusted out long ago, but water pipes are not currently available for purchase by private citizens. For the first time there is talk of reducing the size of the leased property.

In the village people are saying that the householder's son used to bring any number of girls back to the bathing house after a dance or other festivity to spend the night with him, and that the gardener, seated on a bench beneath the eaves of the bathing house, kept watch on such nights to prevent the mistress of the house from discovering these goings-on. People also claim to have heard from the gardener that when this son finally got engaged to a young woman from Berlin, his mother put up the fiancée in the bathing house of all places, so that no one would accuse her of procuring. This gives the village something to laugh about.

After the young householder marries, a daughter is born to the couple, and this baby is scarcely six weeks old when her parents start bringing her to the garden on weekends, and when it is warm enough outside, they place the perambulator with the sleeping infant under the hawthorn tree at the edge of the small meadow. The gardener walks around the property, a burning or already extinguished cigar stump in his mouth, he picks up dry twigs here and there and, when the days grow warmer, he turns on the sprinkler twice a day to water the flowerbeds and meadows, once in the morning and once early in the evening.

When the gardener is no longer able to squeeze shut the handles of the big tree trimming shears, the young woman takes over the task of pruning the shrubs during the spring and summer. The still fruitless trees are finally sawed down by a farmer on the householder's orders and chopped up, the farmer stacks the logs in the woodshed. The gardener now spends many hours sitting, always with one and the same cold stump of a cigar in his mouth, on the threshold of the apiary. The last bees remaining from what were once twelve entire colonies continue to fly about their hives for a little while after the orchard is cleared, then disperse in search of new breeding grounds in the surrounding woods. Sometimes the little girl and her friend from next door sit down beside the gardener, who shows them millipedes and wood lice living in the old logs, and shows them how to make a blowpipe out of the hollow stalks of the elderberry, or whistle with the help of a lilac leaf.

THE VISITOR

THE MAIN THING is that here she can go swimming again. Even if the first time she visits she doesn't know the little pieces of porcelain on the table are for resting one's silverware on between courses. Nor does she succeed in eating her breakfast roll with a knife and fork, which she'd hoped would compensate for her gaffe at lunch the day before. Both misunderstandings produce the same silent smile on the face of her hostess, accompanied by the same light touch of the hostess's cool hand on her forearm. This bread, the hostess says, is so precious that it's perfectly all right to pick it up in one's hands. Back where she comes from she never had to lose any thought over whether or not the bread was precious enough to touch. She'd planted the grain herself, and when she reached out her hands, it was always with the same gesture, from the sowing of the seed to the harvest and baking to the eating of the bread. But here all that is left to do with one's hands is reach out for the finished bread: a skin covering some unknown interior like the Christmas goose with its hidden stuffing. Here in this garden, unlike the garden that belonged to her, there is nothing to sow and nothing to harvest. All one finds here are pines and oak trees with shrubs growing slowly in their shade, the gardener waters the lawn, the flowers are all perennials, and the dill for the potatoes comes from the neighbor woman at the end of the sandy road—the little girl is sent to fetch it from her. Everyone who spends time in this garden does so only in order to be in a garden. Probably she has now reached the right place at the right point in her life, for she too is spending time in her life only in order to be alive. In other places, or so she's heard, old people like her are just stuck up in a tree and left to starve, but nowadays they're even given money to survive on, even if they're no longer able to work. Never will she get used to this money that is given her month after month for doing nothing. In this garden there is nothing left for her to do but sit—sit there in broad daylight with her hands in her lap, watching the larks fly to and fro. Stop dawdling, she hears herself crying out in an inaudible voice as she sits there, stop dawdling, just as she would shout out the kitchen window at her daughter when she was indulging in idle gossip with the girl next door—her daughter was to come inside to do the dishes, scale fish or pluck a chicken. Her daughter always came running, but now her own hands continue to lie motionless in her lap, and as she sits here she can hear her husband playing the accordion—her own parents are silent as their grandchildren babble away—and she answers inaudibly, she offers silent words of consolation or sings without a sound or else just simply goes on saying nothing, and the main thing is that when evening comes she can go swimming again in this shimmering green, cool lake, almost like at home.

It's certainly better, at any rate, to be a stranger among strangers. Once, she had returned from the city they'd fled to at first, walking with her three grandchildren all the way back to the farm, thirty kilometers on foot in the wrong direction, and for a short time had worked as a dairymaid for the Poles who had already taken over the house: she had worked as a maid on the farm that belonged to her. So that her daughter would find her if she were to come back from the labor camp after all. Her little grandson had wanted to dig up the toy tractor he'd buried in a corner of the yard several weeks before when they were leaving, but she wouldn't let him. Her daughter never came back, but the wedding photo she'd always carried with her made its way back into the hands of her mother after various detours, all tattered now and creased, with notations in Cyrillic handwriting on the back. On her way through the garden to the church, her daughter had gotten her veil caught on the red currant bushes and thus had to get married in a torn veil. For the photograph she arranged the veil in such a way that the tear didn't show. Her daughter never came home. And so the mother, who now was only a grandmother, set out again for the second time with her three grandchildren. It's certainly better, at any rate, to be a stranger among strangers than in one's own home.

The dandelions are the same here as back home, and so are the larks. Now, as an old woman, she has grown into the sentence that her husband always said to her forty years before. The dandelions in her village were the same as the dandelions where he grew up, in the Ukraine, from where he'd come vagabonding along, and the larks too, that's what he always said. And in Bavaria, from where his great-grandparents had emigrated to Russia, and to where he'd originally meant to return, without knowing anything more about this homeland than its name, there were surely also such dandelions, such larks. Surely her husband's great-grandparents had at some point or other uttered this very sentence another seventy or eighty years before. She wonders whether the sentences go out looking for people to utter them, or whether it's just the opposite and the sentences simply wait for someone to come along and make use of them, and at the same time she wonders if she really doesn't have anything better to do than wonder about such things, what silliness, she thinks, and then she remembers that she doesn't have anything better to do, she looks at the ottoman on which her crooked legs are propped, it's upholstered in the same red vinyl as the armchair in which she sits. Probably, she thinks, the sentences all get overtaken sooner or later and are spoken by someone or other, somewhere or other, just as everything belongs to everyone among people who are fleeing—factored over the length of a lifetime, the course of both objects and human beings was no doubt no different from the experience of a refugee. In peacetime it was poverty, during the war it was the front that kept pushing people before it like a long row of dominos, people slept in other people's beds, used other people's cooking utensils, ate the stores of food that other people had been forced to leave behind. It's just that the rooms became more crowded the more the bombs fell. Until in the end she arrived here, in this garden, and when the gong calls her to supper, she finds it quite plausible to think that this gong was already calling to her back then, when she turned her back on her farm for the last time and set off again with her three grandchildren, carrying an eiderdown and with a blue-patterned kerchief on her head. When you've arrived, can you still be said to be fleeing? And when you're fleeing, can you ever arrive?

Her husband died before all of this. When she looks back from his death to the accident with the clover press, it seems to her as if his dying had arrived then already, slipping in through a side door without bothering to identify itself. Even the tearing of her daughter's bridal veil was a sort of entrance, through a side door, of what was to be, but since that was still the time when all the rest was yet to come, she couldn't yet recognize it. Now that she is old and living only to be alive, all these things exist simultaneously. Now that she is old, her husband's injury could be the reason she fell in love with him, and the music he played when he arrived in her village had its roots in his early death, and her daughter, on the other hand, was perhaps already sitting beside her there in the oven, holding her hand when she was pregnant with her, she had been locked up in the oven because she'd fallen in love with that vagabond, the father of the child she was carrying. And this, if you looked at it the right way, was surely the reason he'd come vagabonding along, even before he knew her. As she looks back like this, time appears in its guise as the twin of time, everything flattening out. Things can follow one after the other only for as long as you are alive in order to extract a splinter from a child's foot, to take the roast out of the oven before it burns or sew a dress from a potato sack, but with each step you take while fleeing, your baggage grows less, with more and more left behind, and sooner or later you just stop and sit there, and then all that is left of life is life itself, and everything else is lying in all the ditches beside all the roads in a land as enormous as the air, and surely here as well you can find these dandelions, these larks.

You aren't going to marry a man like that, her mother said and locked her up in the oven for several days. But when it turned out she was already pregnant, her mother let her out of the oven again and said: You could have had the postman, the forester, the head fisheries inspector. In order to earn money for his family, her husband had begun to maintain the equipment and machinery of the farmers, including the clover press. From then on he played his music only for his own pleasure and for hers, for the pleasure of his wife. But after he'd cut off four fingers of his left hand on the clover press, he could play neither fiddle nor accordion. Along with his fingers, the clover press had cut off his music from him. This music that he'd played until his accident came from the Ukraine, from where he'd arrived as a vagabond. After his injury, his hand always felt cold, and so she'd sewed a fur-lined mitten that he wore year in and year out from September until well into May. With this mitten on his hand and his hand in his lap, her husband had often sat there in his final years, just as she was doing now, although he was still young. When he died, still in his early forties, she couldn't bring herself to throw away the fur mitten. But when she had to flee, it got left behind in the house.

She can go swimming here just like at home, and swimming has remained easy for her, unlike walking, for which her bones haven't been strong enough for some time now. At night, when she takes down her gray knot of hair before going to bed, her hair is still damp. In summer, when she was young, she swam and dove her way through the Masurian lakes, fished in them too, and in winter she went ice-skating, the blades would be screwed into the soles of her boots. She reached out her hands to touch the waters of these lakes, washed herself in them, drank from them, ate their fish and scratched up their ice, she'd worked over the lakes the way her daughter, who so loved to bake, later worked over the cake dough she would knead four hundred times with both hands before putting it in the oven. To this day her shins are blue and purple from the lace-up boots, which had to be laced especially tight for ice-skating, blue and purple and shiny as stone from the hours and hours of being laced up, hours and hours of racing across frozen lakes that let out dark cries of jubilation beneath the cuts the girl was carving into them with her skates. Now her crooked legs with their shins that still shine blue and purple lie upon the red vinyl of the ottoman, which is intended for one to prop one's feet on, and they are nonetheless still her legs. She doesn't know what the lake here looks like in winter, the mistress of the house keeps referring to the house as her "summer place." In the winter it's just the gardener living in his room, otherwise the house is empty, and then it's closed up for the winter, the shutters are placed over their windows, the night storage heater turned down to its lowest setting. And then everyone leaves for the city. Her husband went fishing even in winter, he was always one of the first on the ice, when it was still cracking, a small, dark figure crouching there at dawn, motionless. In winter they heated their house with wood, they would light the stove with pine shavings, but as soon as the fire was burning well they would switch over to beech and oak, the hard wood burned longer. When the pump in the yard froze solid, they would fetch their water from the lake, from a hole that her husband hacked in the ice near the shore. It's quite possible, she thinks, that ottomans for propping one's feet on were invented only after people had begun to choose their seasons. Invented here, in this season where she will now be a visitor for the rest of her life.

The youngest of her three grandchildren, who had a squint her whole childhood and had to go to school bald her first day because of scabies, this most infelicitous youngest child who fell into the water when trying to jump the creek and came home with her clothes all green, this youngest daughter married the son of the mistress of the house and is now, a towel across her shoulders, clattering down the stone steps to the lake in wooden sandals, humming under her breath and turning to give a quick wave before she disappears behind the large fir bush. Sometimes she sits down beside her grandmother and chats for a bit while painting her toenails red. When her, the grandmother's teeth come unglued during a meal, she feels more ashamed before her granddaughter than the mistress of the house. Back where she learned about growing old from old people, there were no false teeth. When you got old, your mouth collapsed. But nowadays in the place where she is a visitor, even faces are made ready for winter.

Being a visitor isn't easy. In her village it was customary to reject a gift exactly three times before accepting it, and when you accepted it, you yourself brought a present the next time, which the other person would then reject exactly three times before accepting it, and so on. A flowering plant in exchange for strawberries, a bottle of home-fermented wine for a piece of freshly slaughtered pork, apples for pears. To this day her friend, the only one from their village who also wound up in Berlin after the war, brings her a little pot filled with clover every New Year's Eve in which a tiny chimney sweep made of wire is standing, and she herself has just the same sort of little clover pot with the chimney sweep stuck into it as a gift for her friend. The pots with their sweeps are exchanged at midnight, and on New Year's morning her girlfriend carries home the pot she has received as a present in the same bag she used to carry her pot there. Since her granddaughter got married, she has been bringing her, her grandmother, along with her on summer vacations to visit her mother-in-law, and this mother-in-law is approximately the same age as her daughter would be now, the daughter who left for her work detail and remained there for all eternity. And when she, the grandmother, asks her granddaughter what she should bring as a hostess gift, the granddaughter always replies: But you're part of the family. But she isn't so sure she belongs to this family in which she has been warmly received by her granddaughter's mother-in-law for the last five summers now but always greeted using the formal mode of address, always *Sie* and never *du*. This mother-in-law sometimes recommends a salve to help with her rheumatism, asks her about her apartment in Berlin, says she could have this or that dress of hers altered by her seamstress to fit the grandmother, but she has never once called her *du*. For the fifth summer in a row, her granddaughter's mother-in-law uses formal address as she says: Do have a few more potatoes, would you like some more vegetables or a slice of meat, and she doesn't know whether it counts as more polite here to simply say yes or to go ahead and help herself out of the pots and bowls as though she were at home here, or whether she shouldn't, as she would at a stranger's house, say no three times before she accepts. The visitor doesn't understand that her granddaughter's mother-in-law is waiting for her, the grandmother, as the older of the two, to suggest that they call each other *du*.

In fact she even finds it easier to be a stranger among strangers since being a stranger is so familiar to her, she got used to it on one and then the other side of the big gate that separated her farm from the road above. For as long as her family still owned the farm, this big wooden gate was always kept closed unless they were just carting out milk or bringing in the hay. But when suddenly she had cause to seek employment as a dairymaid on her own farm, she knocked on this same gate from the outside and asked the Poles who had meanwhile taken over the farm whether they could hire her. Being at home had already been the first half of this strangeness without her having realized it back then, when she was still at home, chapter one so to speak, and then going away was only the other half, chapter two, strangeness seen from the outside, both halves equal in size, mutually corresponding, but all of it at once—in other words: shutting a gate and being either inside or outside—all of this is very familiar to her. Germany started the war and then lost it, if it had begun it and won, then others would have lost instead. She has learned how to lose; chapter one: having, and chapter two: losing, she kept losing and losing until she'd mastered it. It may be that when one has learned a thing, something else disappears from one's head. When her granddaughter once asked her whether she wasn't sad about it—about the house, the cows, all their possessions—she no longer even understood the question. She had rescued the children, that's all there was to say about it.

She still remembers the stranger who one day, a year or two after the death of her husband but still before the start of the war, had knocked on the gate of the farm. She'd opened it and asked what he wanted. And he had said he wanted to visit his brother, the musician, he'd heard that his brother lived in this village and had even gotten married. The German in which he asked about his brother was antiquated and a little foreign-sounding, just like the German her deceased husband had spoken. No, she'd said, there wasn't any musician here. Could you maybe give me something to drink, he had asked then. And she had left him standing there before the gate and had gone to fetch a glass of milk, she had waited until he'd finished drinking it, then had taken the glass back from him, wished him a good day and closed the gate to the farm again.

The main thing is that here she can swim again.

Back where she comes from, she never had to lose any thought over whether or not the bread was precious enough to pick up in your hands.

In other places, or so she's heard, old people like her are just stuck up in a tree and left to starve.

The main thing is that when evening comes she can go swimming again in this shimmering cool green lake.

Her little grandson had wanted to dig up his toy tractor again.

On her way through the garden to the church, her daughter had gotten her veil caught on the red currant bushes.

The dandelions are the same here as at home, and the larks as well.

What silliness.

When it turned out she was already pregnant, her mother let her out of the oven again.

After his injury, his hand always felt cold.

At night, when she takes down her gray knot of hair before going to bed, her hair is still damp.

The hard wood burned longer.

When you got old, your mouth collapsed.

Apples for pears.

At some point the gong sounds, calling them all to supper. Then her granddaughter comes back up from sunbathing on the dock, humming quietly to herself just as she has done all her life, even as a little girl. Which means that in the end there are certain things you can take with you when you flee, things that have no weight, such as music.

THE GARDENER

IN FALL THE OLD householders invite the gardener to move into the guest room of the main house, this room is on the ground floor, it has its own washbasin and separate entrance, and is easy to heat even in winter with the help of a night storage heater. The gardener accepts the offer. The latest news is that a doctor from Berlin is supposed to be leasing the apiary and erstwhile orchard. While clearing out the shelves in the apiary, the young householder finds a crate filled with silver among the jars of honey. He takes out the silver cutlery and arranges it in the silverware box in the main house. He carries the heating coil, which has been left in the extractor room since the previous winter, back down to the cellar. At exactly the place where a fence once stood, the Berlin doctor has a new fence put up right away, even before the end of autumn, as soon as he's taken possession of the right-hand part of the property. This is not only his right but his duty, since each leaseholder here is responsible for maintaining the property line on the left-hand side as one faces the water. The gardener is able to show the man from the village who is carrying out this work a few of the old border stones that, hidden beneath bushes, can still be detected here and there.

In the village they're saying that since the apiary was torn down the gardener has refused to trim his toenails. According to this rumor, the nails have grown down the front of his toes all the way to the underside of his feet and then up behind the feet to his heels, and even though he hides them inside shoes and socks, you can clearly see by his limping gait that something isn't right. In the village they say that the gardener egged on the householders' little daughter to rip out bunches of grass and throw them along with the dirt clinging to the roots at the freshly plastered house just erected by the doctor from Berlin, and the clumps of dirt thrown by the girl left stains that are still clearly visible. In the village they say that the workers from Berlin who were to drag the bathing house up the hill all showed up for work wearing suits and ties, and that they wore dark-colored windbreakers over their suits as camouflage, information ostensibly provided by the gardener. In the village they say that the new leaseholder of the parcel of land once owned by Jews, this very doctor from Berlin, was to blame for the fact that the senior householder, who went into the hospital with nothing more than a head cold, soon died there. The doctor intentionally gave the man too many shots, they say, because the narrow right of way down to the lake wasn't enough for him, he wanted to have the dock as well, the gardener could certainly attest to this. Finally the gardener, they say, has reported that this Berlin doctor recently, after a celebration in the village pub The Crooked Spruce, went sneaking across his own property with a girl from Frankfurt an der Oder down to the water and from there climbed over the fence so as to make this very dock, the use of which was never granted him by the municipality, the site of an adulterous encounter. The gardener, they say, saw it with his own eyes.

After the death of the old householder, his son, the young householder, leases the workshop as weekend quarters to a young married couple from the district capital who keep their sailboat docked in the village harbor. In exchange, the two agree to regularly mow the lawn on the big and small meadows in summer. The daughter of the young householder and her friend from the neighborhood are allowed to hold the funnel when the gardener helps the subtenants fill the lawnmower with gasoline.

THE SUBTENANTS

YOU HAVE TO DECIDE that on your own, he'd said. And she had said yes. And after this yes she collapsed into a weeping ball without his knowing at first what the matter was. His wife who hadn't even cried the first time she sat across from him in the visitation room at the prison. At the time he had said: I would have sent for you. And she had replied: I know. Nothing more than that. Let alone bursting into tears. Shortly after his release he had then quietly married her. Today, thirty years later, all he had done was say in the course of a conversation: You have to decide that on your own. And she had said something that sounded like "yes," though admittedly the "yes" hadn't been completely clear, and then she had begun to tremble, and since he'd thought she was cold, he'd put his arm around her. On many evenings they'd sat out of doors like that until late at night, side by side on the garden swing beneath the light of the lantern, chatting or in silence, gazing out in parallel lines into the blackness, at the lake whose waves softly lapped in the darkness. Startled by the sound of her crying, he at once withdrew his arm and looked at his wife as he had never before looked at her in thirty years of marriage. Then he got up and walked over to the dock without first, as usual, using his hands to part the branches of the old willow tree that hung down like a curtain above it. So now he stands there, gazing out into the night as his wife continues to sob on the shore behind him. Bawling on the bench, he thinks

111

and can't help grinning. And this grin pulls the corners of his mouth into so wide a grimace that he cannot pull them back again. He stands there on the dock, just at the point where it meets the shore, that place he had stepped to so decisively when his wife had suddenly begun to cry, as though he were striding into a staff dining room or over to the cash register at a department store, not even paying attention to how the branches of the old willow tree scratched against his face, just stands there, grinning out into the night. Lord only knows. Today during the day they'd gone for a sail, the wind was light. She'd held the sheets, he'd hoisted the sails and now and then steered a little.

Sailing is a beautiful thing. Because they loved the water so much, he and his wife had camped out for many years near the harbor before they seized the opportunity to set themselves up here. They were allowed to renovate the workshop down by the water to turn it into a weekend dwelling, but had kept a few useful items such as the workbench with its vice, the shelf for the fishing rods and a small washbasin. Among the nails, ropes and chisels, screwdrivers and rubber boots they had made themselves at home, television, table and bed, everything they needed was here, and now from here they could see their boat bobbing between two buoys near the dock. Sailing is a beautiful thing. After the fall of the Berlin Wall, when the mistress of the house was working abroad and neither she nor her father were taking care of the property, his wife had begun to decorate the small bit of lawn between the shed and the shoreline with stones, had planted asparagus beside the fence and also hung little baskets of flowers from the lower branches of the trees to the right and left of the garden swing, as she had done before in the campground. Beginning in springtime when the boat was put into the water, they would go sailing in virtually all weathers. They might also, for a change, go out in the paddleboat that was hanging on the back wall of the shed. The mistress of the house had given them permission. But they knew nothing more beautiful than just letting the wind carry them along. Sailing is a beautiful thing.

•

When he is sailing, everything seems so quiet. Even when the wind drives into the sails and tugs at the sheets, even then. You don't hear the sound of your own blood either, he thinks, unless you hold your hand to your ear, and he holds his hand to his ear. When they are sailing, he and his wife exchange only the most necessary words. Sailing is like a service. What sort of service he really couldn't say, and just as little does he know who has called for this silence that he and his wife maintain without ever having spoken of it. When he is sailing, the water seems infinite to him. Even when the shoreline is always in view. Even when they sail in circles or from one end of the lake to the other and then back again, over and over. Probably the sense of infinity comes from the motion, he thinks, but this is yet another thing he has never discussed with his wife. Should I call my sister or not, his wife had asked him, and he had said: You have to decide that on your own. Lord only knows. Now the water is lying black before his feet and lapping at the shore, and behind him his wife is sobbing. Perhaps this sobbing is only an inward-turned lapping of the water that is now, as she weeps, running from her eyes and nose, he thinks, and can't help grinning once more. That one time, when he tried to swim to the opposite shore of the river, the water had been so black and had made faint splashing noises like this. He hadn't gotten terribly far that night. Just like today. Today he stands grinning at the end of the dock and is already caught again, already nabbed once more from behind, without ropes—that time just by shouts from the shore, threats and curses, and tonight by sounds, that time without a boat under his rear end, swimming, and tonight standing at the end of the dock. His wife who didn't cry even that first time when she sat across from him in the visitation room at the prison now is crying.

At the time he had known that he had to turn back. His friend hadn't turned back. On this river, where swimming was forbidden, the water flowed downstream just like other rivers, he and his friend had often swum for pleasure in other rivers, had dived down to the bottom or let themselves be swirled around by the current. Still swimming that night, he had felt surprise that this thing that was utterly prohibited here was nonetheless so much like all the other swimming. Even today he knows that sooner or later he must turn back, return to the circle of light beneath the lantern where his crying wife is sitting on the garden swing. When he learned to ride a motorcycle, not even sixteen years old, he practiced together with his friends in a place close by here, on an unfinished bit of autobahn up in the woods, one of those strips of concrete leading from nowhere to nowhere that you could find everywhere in these parts if you knew your way around. A sandy path suddenly turns into highway and then just as suddenly reverts to a path again or else just stops somewhere right at the edge of the woods as if there were a wall. Back then, when he borrowed a motorcycle from an older friend for the first time to practice on this autobahn in the woods, he knew how to step on the gas but had forgotten to ask how to brake. When the autobahn then ended at the edge of the woods as if there were a wall, he had ridden at full tilt into the woods and swerved wildly around the oaks and pines with the wide mirrors his friend had mounted on the handlebars, not knowing how to stop a machine of this sort. Shit, he had thought, and steered and steered, searching for the way out of these woods more with his gut than with his eyes. It never occurred to him to just take his foot off the gas. Sometimes it happens that a joke has a hard seed inside and when he bares his teeth to laugh he finds himself biting down too hard and then he can't let go. Shit. His wife is still crying. Shit, he thinks, standing with his back to her. Whether a single word can itself be a thought is something he doesn't know, but in any case this one word is everything he is thinking, thinking more with his gut than his head. If so, it's probably the sort of thought that suddenly appears without warning, just like the woods he'd gone zooming into that time, and then just as suddenly it's over again. It's just that the route between the oaks and pine trees planted much too close together appears infinitely long when you are swerving between their trunks, and the forest's shade does not cool you as you career through it, instead it burns from within. Shit. When after infinitely many twists and turns he felt the autobahn beneath his tires again just as suddenly as it had vanished before, he was grateful to Hitler for the first time in his life. All the mirrors were still intact.

Turning back, then, is an art he has mastered, or else it's mastered him, Lord only knows. Whether you swim straight ahead or turn back, the swimming is still the same. His friend, with whom he had gotten drunk on that night and then, as if it were just a joke, jumped side by side into the river, did not turn back. Either he hadn't heard the shouts from behind him as he swam, or he took them for part of the joke, or else—and this too is possible—he simply hadn't wanted to turn back. The swimming is always the same. His friend had never reached the opposite shore, or this one either. Sailing, he had practiced flipping the boat with his wife. Make the boat capsize, spin it on a longitudinal axis along with its crew and then right it again. Hold tight to the mast to stay on board as the boat surfaces again. Sailing is a beautiful thing. Lord only knows.

Only for the past week has his wife known she has a sister. One week ago the telephone rang. A friend from school whom the woman had neither seen nor spoken to in thirty or forty years. What a surprise, so you're still, how did you, and who gave you, they're talking about a reunion, no really, and so-and-so, and that girl who, and what's the name of the one who prematurely, oh, so he's already, how terribly sad, and did he, and how many children, work, husband, sailing, weekend property, does she actually have the address, and besides, what ever. Besides, what ever became of your sister. What sister. And is your stepfather still alive. What stepfather. Oh wait, you still don't know, this friend says now, all of this on the telephone, I mean, your father wasn't even, what, the woman says, gazing out at the water, as she holds the receiver to her ear, the sailboat is bobbing near the dock between two buoys, oh, I'm so sorry I, the voice of her friend is now saying inside the telephone receiver, but her husband cannot hear this. Her husband hears only how his wife, after pausing to listen to the telephone, just says: What sister, and a few moments later after a brief pause says: What stepfather. And then finally only says or asks: What? He had laid the telephone cable himself, back before the end of the GDR, running it down from the house all the way to the workshop. The father of the mistress of the house had given them permission to have their own extension off the main line. They themselves had been waiting thirteen years to have telephone service installed in their own apartment in the district capital. If there's a telephone somewhere, it will ring.

My childhood was like something out of a fairytale, his wife had always said to people, smiling. She would then say something about her father, who had showed her how to catch fish, plant asparagus and handle a rake. Her father had always called her his baby girl. When she talked about her childhood, all the people listening to her always looked as if they wished they too had had childhoods like something out of a fairytale. She never spoke of her stepmother. When her father was home, her stepmother had never dared to strike her. She couldn't remember her biological mother, and her father never talked about her. But now, a lifetime too late, she has learned on the telephone that even her father was not real and that besides her there was yet another little girl in a nearby village, her sister, whom she does not remember. Both of them, she and this other little girl, had been brought here as the small children of war refugees from the Giant Mountains on the border of Bohemia and Silesia and then had been given to different parents in different villages, her friend had said. Everyone in the village knew that. Everyone but her. Oh, I'm so sorry I, the friend says.

Should one, a lifetime too late, try to find one's own sister, and if one actually succeeds in finding out where she is living, should one then call her, invite her for a visit or visit her oneself? Write her a letter, or else leave everything as it was before, even if from now on everything will be different? Any older woman sailing past her on a boat might be her sister. Or the madwoman who always pushes around an empty shopping cart in the nearby spa town, mumbling curses. A woman sitting in a café with a piece of cake. An energetic sixty-something seeking a non-smoking man in a classified ad, or else some scrawny old biddy in Berlin. Possibly her sister died ages ago and is already under the ground. Is everyone in the world now related to her, or is it the other way around, everyone once close to her now all at once either a stranger or dead? As a child she had always asked her father when she couldn't make up her mind. Later, too, after her father's death, she would imagine, whenever she wasn't sure what to do, what he would have advised her in this or that situation. But if her father wasn't even her father, who can give her advice? When she'd asked her husband just now whether she should call her sister, he'd just replied: You have to decide that on your own. Now, a lifetime too late, she is on her own. Where should she go if she wants to return to the place where she was actually born? The Giant Mountains?

Only a week before they climbed down into the black river from which he had emerged shortly afterward, dripping and shivering, but from which his friend had not, they had begun to give serious thought to their circumstances. In their course of study, they would soon both be facing exams that neither he nor his friend were going to pass, that much was clear. For various reasons they had used the time they should have spent studying for the exams on other things. His friend had been an organizer for the student carnival, had gone about investigating various locations and written numerous letters until finally the Museum of Natural History had agreed to open up several of its rooms to the party. Dressed as devils and swine, schoolgirls, Romans and mermaids, the students had descended upon the palatial building after closing time and had set up a cold buffet on the glass display cases, then proceeded to dance the night away between dinosaur skeletons and stuffed gorillas, a few of them had tried to drink the alcohol from the display cases diluted with water, others had climbed into the larger dioramas, presenting *tableaux vivants* of love and slumber among the foxes and elks. The organization of this epic party, at which proposals of marriage were made and accepted, and children conceived, had driven every last thought of statistics and structural physics from his friend's head. He himself, on the other hand, while out on one of his forays through the ruins of Berlin, had stumbled upon a catacomb dating from the previous century in whose vaults corpses from the Biedermeier period had been perfectly preserved along with their clothes and headwear. In their coffins they had outlasted the war and all those other, fresher deaths, and although they were shriveled up, they remained clearly recognizable down to their toenails and top hats. He had asked his now wife, who at the time was his fiancée, whether she wouldn't like to keep one of these corpses in her hallway as a sort of valet stand. But his fiancée had thought the entire story was invented and the valet suggestion a joke, and a bad one at that, and therefore she hadn't even laughed. He had then spent many hours down in this crypt sketching the corpses, without of course giving the least thought to the principles of physics that made it possible for a ruin, for example, to remain standing.

We have to get to the West, his friend had said then one evening when there was only a week's time left before the exam. We'll repeat the year there. Students from the East were held back a year when they continued their studies in the West, and that was precisely the year they had lost to their carnival and corpses. A new beginning, his friend had said. Here there was no chance: Here the files on their entire cohort—and along with them time—kept steadily advancing. Then they had thought about where their escape could be undertaken most easily. Neither he nor his friend were familiar with the terrain around the "green" unmarked border, and they didn't have a balloon, so they decided to try the Elbe. It was still so cold, his friend had said, that the border guards wouldn't seriously be expecting anyone to try swimming the river. We'll get drunk first so we don't feel the cold, and then we'll just zip across, his friend, the Saxon, had said. Neither he nor his friend had brought up their women. Although this now appears to him beyond comprehension, he would say that at the moment he had simply forgotten all about his fiancée. One week later they packed up a pipe wrench and three bottles of wine, got on a train with their bicycles, rode the train for an hour and a half, and then from a tiny train station bicycled out to the meadows along the Elbe. There they got drunk in the dark and then, on the eve of their exams in statistics and structural physics, just as planned, they climbed down into the river to swim back a year in time.

The next time he saw his fiancée—today his wife—it was in the courtroom. She had been called as a witness and asked whether she'd known of his intention to flee the country. And she had, quite truthfully, said no. Compared with this moment, all questions regarding structural physics suddenly appeared facile, and it was clear to him that he had swum into his test rather than away from it. The swimming though is always just the same. Later he asked his fiancée to bring him a book about structural physics, he studied the book and then conducted tutorials on this subject for his fellow prisoners. The percentage of men from the construction sector that were sitting in prison just then was higher than usual: During the construction of the Berlin Wall, a number of workers had attempted to reach the other side of the very structure they were building. After serving his time in prison, he went to see his former professor and asked for permission to take the exam even though he was no longer enrolled. He passed with flying colors but never took up his studies again.

Now his wife seems to have grown calmer, he hears glasses clicking together which means she has no doubt gotten up and begun to clear the table. When he turns around he glimpses her through the curtain of willow twigs, she is just disappearing into the toolshed with a tray in her hand. His eyes come to rest on the white hanging baskets made of plastic that she has hung in the trees, these baskets are illuminated by the lantern and in their artificiality appear even further removed from the night than the light itself. The shed in which he and his wife have made themselves at home among the tools stands surrounded by darkness. Their arrangement with the mistress of the house has been only provisionally in effect ever since the heirs of the former owner of this piece of land filed for the return of their property, and so both the vacation quarters themselves and the subtenant relationship are now only makeshifts, as the mistress of the house put it. When the ownership of these heirs has been legally confirmed, they will have to leave, both he and his wife, this is what has been agreed. But when that will be is something no one knows. Subtenant sounds like a euphemism for a sort of weed, his wife had remarked after their conversation with the mistress of the house, and somehow ever since he has associated the notion weed with the happiness he experiences here when he is sailing. Happiness grows out of disorder, just as infinity grows out of the finite lake on which he is now turning his back. He and his wife spend their weekends in a toolshed, tie up their sailboat to a dock that doesn't belong to them, and are nonetheless, he would say, utterly and completely happy on this parcel of land that they have conditionally borrowed.

If he had succeeded in escaping then, he probably would have managed to complete his studies in West Germany. In any case, the Museum for City History had bought his drawings of the corpses right away after the catacombs were opened, the corpses relocated and the church rebuilt. But after his time in prison, as was only to be expected in the East, he had been sent to work in production to purify himself: He was assigned to a furniture factory. In fact this was supposed to be only a transitional position, a makeshift solution. Half a year later he would have been allowed to take up his studies again, even here, but he himself had made the decision to remain in the factory as an ordinary worker. The makeshift had lasted his entire life until now, when it was time for him to retire. Whenever the topic came up in conversation, he would always say that he'd simply realized that he preferred this practical work to his studies. Lord only knows. Feeling the unsteady boards of the dock beneath his footsteps, he thinks that it would be lovely if he and his wife would succeed in dying before the matter of the inherited property was finally settled. Then the person giving the speech at the funeral would be able to say that until the very end they had been able to pursue what they loved: sailing.

THE GARDENER

IN THE VILLAGE they say the daughter of the house has been seen at night sitting with a few boys out on the pier where the steamboat docks, smoking and drinking. Especially when the moon is full she likes to clamber over the railing of the little balcony beside her window with her parents and grandmother none the wiser, she climbs down the window frame of the downstairs window, then steps into the interlaced hands of the gardener held up to assist her, and later she ascends again by the same method.

The subtenants are glad the gardener remains sitting quietly on the threshold with the cold cigar stump in his mouth when they start to saw down the big fir bush, what they're after is to lay the telephone wire in as direct a line as possible from the house down to the workshop so that this cable they have purchased themselves will reach. In any case the fir bush has become yellowed and unattractive in recent years, besides which it's been hollow inside for some time now. When they are removing the huge stump with its roots, they discover a crate filled with porcelain. Not bad, all the things that grow in a garden, the young householder says when they show him the crate. A miracle of nature, he says. The gardener nods. The householder picks up the crate and carries it to his car.

THE CHILDHOOD FRIEND

SOMETIMES HE CLIMBS UP a ladder to straighten the tarp with which he covered the thatch roof of the bathing house the previous fall. Perhaps he would use a similar gesture to draw up the covers at night to tuck in his friend if she were now his wife and lying in bed beside him as had been agreed on so many years ago. On the side facing the lake, the roof has begun to rot. There isn't much sense to what he's doing, it's possible the roof will even rot faster under the tarp, but he still can't bring himself to just abandon the roof to the wind. Under the tarp it will still hold together for a little while longer and look like a roof.

If his father hadn't sent him to run home from the construction site that day to get some beer, he wouldn't have come down the path just as she was picking raspberries with her father on the slope across from their house. Her father had waved him over and asked whether he wouldn't like to have some raspberries too, and he'd said yes. From then on, the first time he plucked raspberries with her, until today, when he climbs up on the ladder to straighten the tarp on the roof of the bathing house, life has taken its course. Sometimes he asks himself whether, if their two fathers had not acted as if in cahoots that day to make them playmates, his life would still have become his life. But life would no doubt have filled up with various other sorts of would-haves and probably been just as much his life as this one. At the time, when he was five years old and she had just turned four, their fathers or who knows who had made a decision once and for all about the gestures with which he now, in his mid-fifties already and perched atop a ladder, is tugging straight a tarp that's gotten rumpled in the wind.

I dare you to crawl out farther on this branch, let's go for a swing, did you know you can smoke cattails, let's use the tiles to build a house in the water, I found a bullet casing, me too, let's go for a swing, if you put a board over the tire you'll have a raft, you have to use elderberry stalks to make a blowpipe, they're hollow on the inside, the gardener said so, let's go to Liedtke Park, it's all wild and there are apples growing that don't belong to anyone, let's go for a swing, c'mere, I'll give you a boost, how far down can you dive, my ship has a rudder made of metal, let's say the bedroom is from the pillow there to the blanket, let's go for a swing, can you ride no-hands, did you know that little boy Daniel got up on the windowsill and peed out the window, oh no, my oar just fell in the water, give me a kiss.

Over there between the roots of the big oak tree that he can see perfectly well from up on the ladder is where they'd buried the little chest that contained, as treasure, the aluminum pennies from his sister's wedding, and when they dug the hole they found the pewter pitchers that someone else had put in the ground at exactly that spot. When he stands on the ladder now, he isn't looking at the roots of the oak tree, but presumably the little chest is still there in the ground, or, if it's rotted since then, at least the pennies are still there. Did you know that Daniel is dead? Did you know he died even before his father tried to shoot his mother dead? Do you remember how he used to go diving with us, among the pikes in the reeds, and how cold the pikes were when they bumped our legs with their fish mouths? Not long after the border was opened, he went diving in the Caribbean and drowned. No, really. As if opening the border just gave him more possible ways to die. The trip was his would-have. Now he'll be a little boy forever. After the night when Daniel's father, who had cancer and was on his deathbed, shot at Daniel's mother, she too lay on her deathbed. No, really. As if dying in such a family just eats its way through everything. Did you read the newspapers when for days the front page showed the bungalow where Daniel peed out the window that time? Now the window is dark and empty, the whole bungalow has been dark since the shooting. They say the argument was about the bungalow itself. Daniel's father shot at Daniel's mother from the bed. It was about the inheritance for Daniel's younger half-brother. The one from the West. No, really. So opening the borders apparently also gave Daniel's parents more possible ways to die.

In order to stretch the tarp over the roof last fall, he had set foot on the property of his childhood friend for the first time since helping her pack up and empty out the house years before. He hopped over the little wall made of fieldstone and worked his way through the bushes because the gate he'd always entered as a child was locked now. He had sat with her on the bricked pillars to either side of the gate so they could stick their tongues out at passers-by. When he now thinks back to that weekend when she emptied out and left the house, or even to his visit in Berlin when he was fourteen years old, or, even further back, to that afternoon in the woodshed when she and he had seen something it would have been better for them not to see, it strikes him as strange that, independent of what is happening, one day is always followed by another, and to this day he doesn't know what it actually is that is continuing. Perhaps eternal life already exists during a human lifetime, but since it looks different from what we're hoping for—something that transcends everything that's ever happened—since it looks instead like the old life we already knew, no one recognizes it. The house too is still standing there, and he doesn't know what it is that is still standing. And he himself. And no doubt she as well, somewhere in the world.

At our house we have gooseberries and currants and apples in the garden, but the gooseberries and currants are already done for the year, he'd said, and her father had given him permission to show her his garden that afternoon. At our house there are just roses, she'd said when she stood there in his garden, then she bit into an unripe apple. That is when what he now, in retrospect, would call his childhood first began, from vacation to vacation it would begin when she arrived and end when she departed. On the day when his sister stepped out onto the road in her wedding dress to walk to the church to be married, and a pot of pennies was dumped out over her for luck, and afterward he and his friend picked all the lightweight coins from the sand, aluminum money that weighed almost nothing—on that day, while the wedding party was already drawing farther away and they were still dragging their hands through the pale sand, she and he had spoken for the first time of marriage.

You can break open hazelnuts with a heavy stone, they're still white on the inside, let's go for a swing, I can ride around the puddle to the left with my front wheel and to the right with the back one, let's make up a secret language, kissing should be called twittering, no really, let's go for a swing, you can't talk while you're fishing, squeeze the lilac leaf all the way flat between your hands, that's how it makes the best whistle, the gardener said so, let's go for a swing, c'mere, we'll bury the mole under the tree right here, you can eat the little hearts on the shepherd's purse, let's go hide under the fir bush, give me a—I want to twitter, me too.

His parents always left the house early, at six in the morning, at eight his friend had breakfast, at eight-thirty he was allowed to come over. On cool mornings, the handle of the gate with the pillars to the right and left of it still had dew on it when he pressed it down. As he walked past the kitchen window, he would knock on the greenish panes so that the cook would unlock the door for him, then he would go inside and wait in the living room next to the long table at which his friend and her family and the friends of her family were sitting, he would stand there, leaning up against the cold stove, waiting until she finished eating. Afterward they would play in her garden or his, go swimming from his or her dock, hide in the secret closet in her room under the coats and dresses or go to his house, where the television would be on even during the day, and watch the black and white cowboys galloping across a black and white plain and eventually their black and white falling down and dying.

He'd read once that embryos in the womb go through all the stages of evolution, that they begin as fish and amphibians, and later get fur, then for a while have the spinal columns of pigs and only afterward are born as human beings. Perhaps, he thinks, a second primeval era begins after birth, this time the speeded-up history of mankind but now going under the name of childhood, as if the time of the hunter-gatherers had to be shared by everyone once more, as the basis from which the various sorts of adults could develop. After all, fish and amphibians gave rise, in the course of evolution, to a large variety of creatures, some had developed into land animals which in the end became monkeys and cats, and others chose to spend their lives in the water and later became dolphins or whales. If this is how things were, then he had made her acquaintance in the Stone Age and shared his life with her until approximately the late Middle Ages, and after all this was a period lasting two and a half million years.

Perhaps—at least this is how it looks to him today—such a primeval era that two people spend together is a more indissoluble bond than a promise would be. The eyes with which he and she saw something that day in the woodshed that it would have been better for them not to see, are still right there in their heads after all, even though these heads are meanwhile, seen in purely spatial terms, far removed from one another. The seeing from that day still persists. In the woodshed, he and she had made themselves a hiding place up on top of all the wood, in the one meter of space remaining between the stacked logs and the roof of the shed. They had used logs to divide the space up there into rooms, lined the rooms with leftover bits of carpet, here and there nailed scraps of cloth to the wood, and hung up a flashlight to provide illumination—and so, crawling around, they had a whole apartment to keep house in. From his ladder, he can see the roof of the woodshed, which meanwhile is entirely covered with the leaves and dry branches that have fallen. *My cousin, Nicole, is here for a visit, she always wants to go swimming naked, and she even lets me kiss her when she's naked.* René, the nephew of the director of the State Combine for Automobile Tires, was a bit older than they were, the child of vacationers, and whenever he was there, he would always come looking for them in the shed and crawl up to sit with his head ducked down in their hiding place, full of suggestions of things they should try. *My cousin, Nicole, is here for a visit, she always wants to go swimming naked, and she even lets me kiss her when she's naked, she's only twelve like you, but I'm sure she'd sleep with me too.* Every electrical outlet has three cables, a blue one, a red one and a yellow one. The blue and red ones are necessary for the electricity to flow, and the yellow one, even though it's never connected anywhere, is there too, and it's called the ground. *My cousin, Nicole, she always wants to go swimming naked, and she even lets me kiss her when she's naked, she's only twelve like you, but I'm sure she'd sleep with me too. If you hide behind the wood, you can watch, do you want to?*

By this time they'd long since learned what it looks like when blood flows out of a cut, they had even sliced open their own arms with a pocket knife so they would be blood brothers, and they also knew what it looks like when a person shits and the sausage first starts coming very slowly out of the hole and then quickly pops out and falls, under the willow tree beside the water first he, then she had squatted down so that the other could watch. And since seeing had always only been seeing, neither touching nor smelling nor tasting nor even hearing—for hearing, your hand would still vibrate when you held it to the cloth cover of the radio's loudspeaker—since seeing itself could never be filled with even the tiniest bit of reality, the storerooms behind their eyes had, at the time, seemed infinitely large to both of them, and that was no doubt why both she and he immediately responded to their neighbor's suggestion by saying yes.

Of course they could have given a nudge to the pile of logs separating them from the bedroom of their hiding place when René asked his cousin Nicole if she knew how children were made. Even somewhat later, as René was explaining this to his cousin Nicole, who didn't yet know about it, they might still have burst suddenly out of hiding and declared it all one big joke. But when René, who was already somewhat older, asked Nicole whether she wouldn't like to try out what he had just been explaining to her and she said no, and then kept saying no again and again while he held her down and used his body to press her legs apart, and both of them were still naked from swimming, and when Nicole, who was only twelve and weaker than René, who was already going to be starting an apprenticeship after this summer, started crying, and he held her mouth shut and then began to jerk back and forth on top of her, he and she were still watching through the tiny slit that allowed them enough space between the logs to see everything that was happening. First it had been too soon to burst out of hiding, and then it was too late, and the dividing line between too early and too late was so sharp that it couldn't even have been called a no man's land. Behind the wooden wall where René had walled in the two seers, it was dark and cramped, and if they had so much as shifted position, everything would have collapsed.

They saw. They saw so long and so much that all the storerooms behind their eyes were filled with what it would have been better not to have seen. He has no memory of how he and his friend later crawled out of their hiding place, how they climbed down the variously tall piles of wood and escaped to freedom. If you had to go by what a person remembers, he would consider it possible that they never did get back outside again but were still squatting to this day beneath the roof of the shed, which meanwhile is entirely covered with the leaves and dry branches that have fallen. That one can be more thoroughly tied to a place through shared cupidity and shame than by shared happiness is something he wishes he'd never had to learn.

There was only one thing that he couldn't understand at the time: that his friend only ever spent her vacations in the place where he lived. He lives there still, even though his hands are starting to turn into the hands of an old man. Only after his coming-of-age ceremony when he visited her in Berlin, on that one special weekend not long after his *Jugendweihe,* the one single time when the direction was reversed, when he was the one making the journey and she the one who lived there, had he understood, but by then it was too late. *You sunshine of my heart,* one of her schoolmates had written to her, always the same form of address: *You sunshine of my heart,* and then all sorts of other things on little scraps of paper that she kept in her pencil case. She laughed at him when he found the notes by accident one day and asked who else besides him was allowed to call her the sunshine of his heart. That was just someone kidding around, she said, just a joke, but when he didn't let up and wasn't prepared to start laughing, she became annoyed and for the first time ever she said aloud something that apparently had already been self-evident to her even then but to him was not at all self-evident, even now: that when she was in Berlin, which was where she lived, she could do whatever she liked.

From that point on it was never again possible for him—neither during her next vacation stay nor any of those that followed—to wait for her beside the long table while she sat eating breakfast with her family, suddenly he saw himself as a servant standing there, like someone serving himself up on a platter from head to foot with parsley in his mouth and a baked apple stuffed between his toes. Would you care to eat me, madam? From then on the amphibian he had been up till then had chosen a life on land, and the amphibian that she was chose a life in the water, or the other way around, in any case the result of her late-Medieval evolution was that at some point or other, without her ever having to explain anything more to him, she showed up at his door with a male friend, a friend she wanted to introduce to him, her childhood friend, as she now described him. He, her childhood friend, had stood there in the doorway of his house with a plug made of a torn-off bit of tissue sticking out of his nose, because just before she had knocked on the door he had suddenly gotten a nosebleed and had doctored himself provisionally in this way. The knock she had used on his door was still the same secret knock they had used as children. He had opened the door and seen his friend standing there with her companion. Good day, would you like to come in. The friend from Berlin had looked at the bloody snippet of paper sticking out of the nose of his girlfriend's childhood friend. I don't want to disturb you. Later she didn't knock on his door so often when she walked by his house in the company of one or the other boyfriend she'd brought out to the country with her, but when she saw his legs sticking out from under a car in the workshop he had set up next to his house, she would always shout out a greeting to him. When eventually she had married one of these boyfriends, it gradually, over the years, became self-evident that he would help her husband drag the rowboat out of the water in winter and turn it upside-down, hang the paddleboat on the rear wall of the woodshed, and in springtime help the subtenants put up the dock, and occasionally, when she and her husband had no time to come out to the country, he would even clip the hedge, rake the leaves and take care of all the other tasks for which the gardener was now much too old. The hourly wage they paid him was far higher than what was customary in the region.

•

Can you grab that box of books, sure, but I still have my left hand free, here are the shoes, OK, the coffee grinder is staying here, sure, makes sense, it's all rusted anyhow, I laid out the clothing and coats from the closet on the bed, they won't fit in any of the suitcases, they'll have to be hung up, no problem, have you got the bed linens, yes, then just leave the key for the wall cabinets in the lock, who knows if someone else will ever need it, what does it matter, did you go down to the cellar to turn off the electricity and water, no, we'd better not, in case the gardener ever turns up again after all, and close the shutters in the bathing house, OK I'll run down there, but leave the paddleboat where it is, I told the tenants they can take it if they want. The towels, what should I do with them, give them away if you don't need them, can you give me a hand with this lamp, that's all that will fit, you're probably right.

When she moved out, the house still belonged to her and her father since they weren't allowed to sell it as long as the question of its ownership was still up in the air. It belonged to her and to her father, and the telephone still worked. The electricity and water had been turned off when the speculator whom her father had engaged to invest the property for him interrupted the renovation work and left the house to its own devices—but if she had returned, she would have been able to start everything back up again with just a few simple adjustments. Only much later did this speculator call him again to ask him to dig up the soil of the road beside the house and cut through the electrical cable, and to dismantle the water line as well so that her father wouldn't be responsible for the costs that might arise if someone were to decide to install himself in the empty house. Only the telephone line was left undisturbed, since the subtenants had, with her father's permission, run an extension cable down to the workshop.

By doing work of this sort on the properties all around the lake, he'd sometimes made some extra income on the side in recent years. It used to be people had looked down on clandestine employment—"shoddy" was the word automatically assigned to such labor: additions to buildings made without permits and so forth—but now the shoddy work to be done was generally a matter of closing things up and tearing things down. Before this he had, at the request of Daniel's half-brother, dug up the sandy road in front of Daniel's bungalow to cut the electrical cable and disconnect the water supply. After the Schmeling house burned down, he helped with the clean-up operation, and the property suddenly became very cheap after the fire, but still not cheap enough for him, and at his age it wouldn't have been worth it, in any case, to buy an undeveloped property, and he didn't have anyone to leave it to. The next storm will rip the tarp back off the roof again, because it just isn't possible to drive nails into straw—what he is tying to the roof of the bathing house with string is as shoddy as it gets, he thinks as he pulls the strings taut. When a decision has been made about his own house—for here too someone has filed a claim for the restitution of the property—he will find himself a small apartment in the district capital, something with central heating, convenient to shopping and not too expensive.

THE GARDENER

ON THE WEEKENDS in winter when they come out to ice-skate, the subtenants see the footsteps of the gardener in the snow, they start at the guest room and lead sometimes here, sometimes there, crisscrossing the two upper meadows and also passing through the front garden and out the gate, but the prints make clear that none of these paths has been followed more than once. When they run into the gardener, which seldom happens, they ask if he needs something they can bring him next time they come—fresh bread from the baker in the village, eggs, noodles, fruit or something to drink. But the gardener always declines, he shakes his head and goes on his way, a cold cigar stump in his mouth. In the village they say that after the fall of the Berlin Wall the subtenants sold the genuine Meissen porcelain for cheap to buyers from the West. In the village, they say that the gardener has, for some time now, eaten nothing but snow.

When the mistress of the house arrives from Berlin to clear everything out for the investor, the gardener is not there. In his room, the table, chair and bed are as always, a few pieces of clothing have been tossed over hooks, and his rubber boots still stand in one corner, but the gardener himself is not there. The subtenants don't know what to say when asked his whereabouts, they haven't run into him for some time either; recently he's been having more and more trouble walking, particularly downhill. Could something have happened to him? No, the subtenants respond, they don't think so. Together with the mistress of the house and her friend from the village, they search the property from top to bottom looking for him, finally even checking along the shoreline as well. In any case, it's obvious he is nowhere in the house.

The gardener is never seen again, and so two months later the mistress of the house and her father finally consent when the investor urges them once more to build a wall separating the gardener's damp room from the main house to at last put a stop to the dry rot that has established itself there and begun to spread.

THE ILLEGITIMATE OWNER

CLAIM: SURRENDER AND CLEARANCE of the land and house in exchange for compensatory payment to be rendered. Counterclaim. Whether acquisition was in good faith and *in rem* right of use and enjoyment exists is not relevant to the matter under dispute. Civil code of the Federal Republic of Germany, paragraph 985, plaintiff's basis for claim. Undisputed. Actual possession. Actual possession means: Something is under a person's control. Civil code, paragraph 17. As additionally the court may choose not to rule on whether you are entitled to payment as a result of third parties in full knowledge of the claim for restitution having undertaken utilizations of the property, and given the exclusion of a right of retention due to the nature of the creditor claim. Entitlement of counterclaimant on the basis of action under law of unjust enrichment may exist in the amount of the difference between the current market value of the real property and the value without the additional investments. The point of time at which these utilizations were undertaken. Conciliation proceedings. Reference to the registry of deeds will be required to determine with sufficient certainty. Registry of a first priority property lien. In the present settlement. Further: Upon fulfillment of the present settlement all claims with regard to the object of dispute are hereby. Further: All claims with regard to the object of dispute are hereby satisfied and further litigation is hereby. Is hereby excluded.

•

And now she wants to go into the house one more time. With the key still hanging on her keychain, the key with which all the doors in the house and also the woodshed can be opened and closed, this worn-out patent key, Zeiss Ikon brand, which she should have turned in officially two days ago now, with this key she wants to unlock, one last time, the door whose lock always sticks after the first half-turn of the key. The door's glass panes make a faint clinking sound, brittle splinters of red and black paint fall to the ground from the iron tendrils protecting the glass. First she lifts the door a little the way she always does so that the key will continue to turn, then opens the door wide until it hits the wall of the house, pushes the stone in front of it that is still sitting there ready for use, and goes inside.

The painted door to the broom closet has been removed from its hinges, so the first thing she sees when she walks into the house is not, as before, the Garden of Eden in twelve square chapters but rather an old broom, a hand brush, a shovel and a few rags. The door to the living room is off its hinges as well, and so she doesn't have to press down the brass handle to go in, and no metallic sigh is heard when she enters the room. Nine years before, everything made of wood on or adjacent to the two walls affected by dry rot had to be taken down or torn out, and so the long bench seat from along the wall is missing. Workers carried the matching table and the two doors out to the bathing house. The bathing house was too small for the table, so they set it on end, which is how it is still standing today, she glimpsed it through the crack in the shutters as she came in. The key to the bathing house is still hanging in its usual spot on the key board beside the key to the workshop, and the workshop key still has the golden spoon lure dangling from it as usual, and the key board is hanging, as usual, around the corner next to the heating stove, except that now the stove is gone, and the wall it stood against is rotting. The dry rot spread all the way upstairs while she was abroad for work, and her father spent an entire autumn, winter and spring negotiating with the gentleman whom he had offered the right to speculate on the house, which still officially belonged to them, in exchange for carrying out the urgently needed repairs. They weren't allowed to sell it as long as the official decision regarding the restitution claim was still pending, but after all the East German bank accounts were cut in half, they no longer possessed the means to keep up the house themselves. Present exigency: The property that is the object of the proceedings. Pending determination of ownership. Registration number 654.

Her father had never much cared for nature, even in earlier years he'd only ever pronounced the word "nature" with a certain contempt, and he always said he hated mowing the lawn, was bored by flowers, and found swimming utterly uninteresting, only on rare occasions would he dive among the reeds to hunt pike with his harpoon. And so it hadn't surprised her when, after the death of her father's mother, he immediately added her as co-owner to the title of the house—deletions are marked by placing vertical lines above the first and beneath the last line to be deleted and connecting the two lines on the diagonal from upper left to lower right. It hadn't even surprised her that he didn't make even a single trip out to the property after the heirs to the wife of the architect, all of them living in the West, had filed to have the ownership of the land restored to them, nor did it surprise her that he didn't participate in clearing out the house after he had finally reached an agreement with the speculator. Her childhood friend, who helped her clear it out, had been the one to notice the dry rot. One single time during all the many years when the house then stood empty, while she and her father were waiting for the official ruling, he said something to her that she had never before heard from him, namely that every time he found himself having to look at a landscape like this somewhere, a landscape full of hills and lakes, he felt much the same way he felt whenever he heard someone speaking Russian, the language of the country in which he was born. What exactly he meant by this was never explained. She knew only that by the time he got out of the children's home his parents had sent him to because they believed in collective education, he was old enough to mow the lawn. Nature.

The drainage pipe is choked with roots. Six trees have to have their branches removed. The legal right of use has shared the fate of the contract of sale for the property: Neither has gone into effect. Conferred. Nullified. Defunct. The enforcement authority is unable to determine the appropriate settlement amount on the basis of approved methods of investigation. The amount along with the interest accruing during pendency of the proceedings. Effective both retroactively and in the future.

The speculator had gotten rid of the dry rot, installed a new roof, torn out the old bathrooms with the intention of renovating them from the ground up, walled off the gardener's room that had become extremely damp, and broken through the wall to the garage to gain an additional room—but then, when his hopes of coming to an agreement with the heirs and therefore of being able to acquire the house proved illusory, he had the electrical cable severed and left the house as it was. It has been a long time since she last spoke with her father about the property. Leg. Sect. III, No. 1, encumbrance of the land, plot, parcel, property line. Property subject to dispute. Without possibility of appeal.

The stairs leading to the upper floor are covered with dust, bits of plaster from the vaulted ceiling have fallen on the steps and broken apart, and even upstairs the once gleaming cork floor is now covered with a uniform layer of dust. Existing structures in ramshackle condition, actionable. All that remains of the bathroom is the window with its brightly colored squares, the sink, shower, toilet and tiles are gone, now she can look right through the beams supporting the floor down into the hall at the approximate location where her grandmother used to sit on television evenings in the most comfortable of the garden chairs in consequence of her exalted personal status. In the Little Bird

Room where she had slept during all the summer vacations of her childhood—petition after petition opposing clearance of the property under dispute—she now opens the heavy door of the hidden closet—unlawful trespass—the secret door of her childhood whose little wheels draw a semicircle in the dust, on the clothes rod are the bare hangers she herself left behind when she vacated the house. She can now walk through the interior of the large closet directly into the cupboard-lined room used by her grandparents, the wall that once separated these spaces now being absent—lacking the qualifications to acquire this permit, this ruling will remain in effect regardless of future changes in ownership, breach of jurisdiction. The closet through which she enters the cupboard room still smells, just like during her grandmother's lifetime, of peppermint and camphor. In her grandmother's study the ceiling has been eaten away by the feces and urine of the martens, on the desk lie reeds from the thatch roof, and through a hole in the ceiling you can look up into the darkness. The curtains in the windows are secured in their tracks only in a few last spots, the rest of the fabric hangs down askew, trailing loosely in the dust. The window frames are so warped they can no longer be opened. Existing permeabilities. Future permeabilities. Secondary motion is hereby rejected because it contains non-executable and therefore inadmissible provisions. Objection. As opposed to a bona fide. Provided the underlying assumptions have been dismissed. Burden of proof.

Without even having to stop and think, she begins to sweep the reeds from the desk, then goes downstairs again to fetch broom, dustpan, hand brush and rags. In her grandmother's study, in the cupboard room, in the hallway and the Little Bird Room she first sweeps the spider webs from the corners and then from the windowpanes, then wipes the dust from the moldings of the wainscoting, then sweeps the floor, one room after the other, filling the old bucket she found in the kitchen with the dust, debris, reeds and marten feces scattered here and there. Still sweeping the stairs, she descends step by step and dumps out the contents of the overflowing bucket under the bushes. Then she walks, swinging the empty bucket in her hand, between the two meadows and past the big oak tree, taking the path down to the water. Half a year ago she'd had to give the subtenants notice after the bit of shoreline in question had been reassigned to the Jewish parcel to which apparently it once belonged. The dock, therefore, is still standing disassembled in the area before the workshop—but since the fence has not yet been rectified, she nonetheless goes to the old spot, where the path that used to lead to the dock now has only its torso remaining, and squats down there to scoop water from the lake. With one hand she steadies herself against the willow tree, with the other she drags the bucket over the bottom, then she returns to the house and begins to mop the floor upstairs. Five times she has to go down to the lake for fresh water before all the rooms are clean, and with a certain amount of effort she now succeeds in at least opening the balcony door in the Little Bird Room so that the floor will dry more quickly. Through the open window, warm summer air enters the house, and when she steps out onto the balcony, everything is just as she always knew it. Sunlight is falling on the pine tree closest to the house, announcing a beautiful day.

There's more to be done downstairs, because here the stove was torn out, the wall to the garage was broken through to provide direct access, and the gardener's room was walled off. For this reason, washing all the windows is more than she can manage today. In the evening she cranks down the black shutters on the ground floor using the mechanism concealed inside the wall, locks the door from the inside and lies down to sleep upstairs in the closet of the Little Bird Room. The next day she washes the windows, the day after that she carries the doors up from the bathing house and hangs them back on their hinges, she even drags the table, which is very heavy, across the meadow and terrace into the house and puts it back in the hall where it always used to stand. She finds the chairs with the carved initials in the garage, but the leather cushions that go with them are moldy. She starts making it a habit to park her car up at the edge of the main road, and from there she walks down the slope of the Schäferberg, winding her way between underbrush and raspberry bushes, and crosses the sandy road when no one is in sight. She never encounters any neighbors—either their houses have already been torn down or they are standing empty just like hers. Once, on a rainy day, she watches from the Little Bird Room as her childhood friend crosses the big meadow and goes down the hill, returning shortly afterward with the long ladder that still hangs on the back wall of the workshop and props it against the roof of the bathing house. He climbs the ladder, adjusts the tarpaulin that was stretched across the rotting thatch of the roof but has gotten tangled in the wind, and ties it fast at the corners.

On the morning when the real estate agent brings clients to the house for the first time, she has fortunately not gotten up yet and is still asleep in the closet, where she has also been storing her provisions and a few spare pieces of clothing to change into. She doesn't wake up until the real estate agent reaches for the brass knob of the shallow outer door in which the mirror is set, opens the shallow door for her clients and says: And here is a mirror. She hears the clients running their hands over the bird's eye maple veneer, saying: Too bad it's gotten warped. You could have it repaired, the real estate agent says, and now, apparently with some effort, she tugs open the door to the balcony and says: And look what a view you have from here. The clients say: A bit overgrown. The real estate agent says: This here is definitely the better side of the lake—after all, sunsets are always in the West, she laughs, her clients don't laugh, and besides, says the real estate agent, the properties on the other side are separated from the lake by the promenade. They don't have direct access to the water? No, the real estate agent says, at least most of them don't. She says: Just look at the bird here on the railing. Hm, the clients say. It's a loving touch, the real estate agent says. The clients don't respond. The architect, says the real estate agent, worked with Albert Speer on the Germania project. Really, the clients say, now that's interesting.

Then the real estate agent and her clients walk across the hall to the cupboard room, and there too she can hear everything that is said, as there is only a thin door separating her from the people. The real estate agent says: They don't make built-ins like this anymore. That's true, the clients say, but something smells funny, it smells of cats or martens. I've never seen a marten in this house, the real estate agent says with a laugh and then walks on ahead into the study, the milk glass panes inset in the door make a faint clinking sound, and the clients apparently follow, since things now quiet down, some time later the little group returns, the real estate agent is still laughing or again laughing, is this house actually protected as a historic landmark? No, unfortunately not, says the real estate agent, the clients cough, then all of them go back downstairs, and only after absolute quiet has been restored does the former mistress of the house emerge from the closet and look out the window of the Little Bird Room to where the real estate agent and her clients are now walking through the garden, sometimes they stop short, pointing in one or the other direction, for example at the big oak tree that has recently lost one of its largest limbs, or at the roof of the bathing house, they walk slowly as they continue their conversation with a nod or shake of a head until they stop short again here or there to discuss something or other in greater detail.

Following this first visit by the real estate agent and her clients, a wrinkly waterproof cloth now flutters before the kitchen window, bearing the words: For Sale. Along with a telephone number, white against dark blue. Sometimes when it's windy the cloth tugs at its ropes so forcefully you can hear it inside the house. Later one of the cords supporting the sign comes loose, and then the illegitimate owner sometimes sees the cloth being blown inside out as she is trudging down the slope of Shepherd's

Mountain, it slaps itself in its white-lettered face and then sinks back down again.

The house is now so empty that it wouldn't weigh much if she were to order it to rise up in the air and float away. The light coming in through the colored windows would accompany the house on this journey, as would the gleam of the floor that has finally been waxed again and the creaking of the stairs at the second, fifteenth and second-to-last steps. Now she thinks of how her grandmother had the bathing house moved that time, she and her childhood friend had followed the workers all the way up the slope: Complete with its thatch roof, windows and shutters, with its awning and the two wooden columns, it had been pulled slowly uphill between the alders, oaks and pines, and when it then stood in its new location at the top of the hill, the view of the lake you now had from its covered entryway was almost more beautiful than before. But now she no longer knows what direction to float off in.

Many more times, as the summer gradually draws to a close, she stands in the Little Bird Room observing the real estate agent out in the garden with this or that client, one client knocks the toe of his shoe against one of the flagstone steps, to check whether the step is wobbly, another one has the real estate agent show him the cesspit, a third jiggles the fence to the next-door property whose posts have rotted, and keeps jiggling it until two of the posts, held together now only by the wire mesh, lean to one side. Since the house and the land are not cheap, she hears a great many more conversations, many more times the shallow closet door is opened, many times the better side of the lake is mentioned, along with Albert Speer, the cats and the martens. Laughter. Is the house protected as a historical landmark? It isn't. Laughter and coughing. Since the real estate agent is not showing the house exclusively, and it might always happen that one or the other member of the group of heirs to the property might come to check that everything is in order, making the journey from Austria, Switzerland or the Western part of the Federal Republic, or since workers might be sent, or some acquaintance drop by to take a look at things, the real estate agent is not surprised when she doesn't always find everything exactly as she left it the last time she showed the house.

What is it you want, her husband always said to her when she—now the illegitimate owner—spoke with him about the property: You had your time there. She had been unable to explain to her husband that from the moment it first became apparent that she would not grow old in this house, her past had begun to send out its tendrils everywhere behind her, and that although she had long since become an adult, her beautiful childhood had begun, all these many years later, to outstrip her, growing far taller than she was—it was turning into a beautiful prison that might lock her away forever. As if with ropes, time was tying this place down right where it was, tying the earth down tightly to itself and tying her to this earth, and as for her childhood friend—whom she hadn't seen in over nine years now and would probably never see again—it was tying the two of them together forever.

She hears the car doors of the new owners slam shut outside on the sandy road, then the car door of the real estate agent, and finally the car door of the architect. The real estate agent has only come along with them in order to take down the waterproof banner she had mounted outside the kitchen window. This time the real estate agent no longer has to walk through the house with her clients, who are now called the new owners, and she no longer has to utter her sentences, for which she, after having had to say them so many times, will now finally receive within the next ten days her commission in the amount of 6% of the purchase price plus VAT. The new owners and their architect do not enter the house either, instead they walk across the big meadow and from there point first at the lake and then at the bathing house and finally at the place where the house is standing.

Never has the sense of peace inside the house been greater than on the day when, for the last time, she dusts, sweeps, mops and waxes the floors, the day when she opens, one last time, all the windows that can open so as to let fresh air into the house, and then closes the windows one last time, transforming the daylight one last time into light that is green and in parts also dark blue, red and orange, this day on which she draws shut the curtains she has washed in lake water and then hung back up again, closes the door with the milk-colored panes that leads to the study, just as her grandmother had always done when she was writing, and then, withdrawing even further, she also closes the door that leads to the cupboard room. While her grandmother was still on her deathbed and not yet dead, she had picked out her prettiest nightdress, washed it and ironed it so that when the time came she would be ready to give it to her dead grandmother to take with her on her journey. The gentleman from the funeral home had promised to put it on her and to take a photo of her grandmother's corpse in her pretty nightdress during her laying-out. Surely, then, the funeral director had dressed the deceased in her lacy nightdress before cremating the body, surely he had taken the photo and surely put it for safekeeping in some drawer in his office. In her dreams recently she has often seen her grandmother lying in state before her—strangely with an Indian face. That probably had something to do with the fact that in one of the newspapers she'd used to polish the windows she'd read that among the Aztecs sweeping was considered a sacred act.

Now she closes the door to the Little Bird Room, then closes the door to the bathroom that no longer has a floor, and now she goes down the stairs that creak at the second, the fifteenth and the second-to-last step, closes the black shutters with the crank concealed inside the wall, then closes behind her—still with-drawing—the living room door whose handle gives off a metal-lic sigh, closes the door to the kitchen, returns bucket, broom, cloth, hand brush, dustpan and scrub-brush to their places and closes the closet door which, she'd always believed as a child, really led to the Garden of Eden, then she steps outside and fi-nally locks the front door of the house, although she doesn't un-derstand how this can be possible since everything she is now locking away lies so deep within the interior, while the part of the world into which she is withdrawing is so far outside. She locks the door and then walks past the giant rhododendrons to the left of the house, "Mannesmann Air Raid Defense" is writ-ten on the bars that cover the cellar windows, she unlocks the gate, locks it again behind her, exits the front garden through the little gate in the fence and puts the worn-out key in her pocket, even though soon the only thing it will be good for is to unlock air. The balance to be paid out to me. Beyond the reach of law. Document bundle B 3. We request acknowledgment.

EPILOGUE

IN THE CASE OF *this demolition—as with all the others being carried out in this country according to the legal regulations currently in effect—two things are of utmost importance. First, every company that performs demolitions is required to remove all installed fixtures whether they be made of wood (window frames, doors, built-in cabinets, paneling, stairs), metal (radiators, pipes, bars) or, where present, wall-to-wall carpeting, and to dispose of it selectively, that is, sorted by kind, so that the contaminants released through emissions during the demolition itself will be kept to a minimum. The exception is that when window frames are removed, the glass is to be knocked out of them inside the house and left there to be discarded along with the rest of the construction waste since it too is of mineral origin.*

Secondly, care should be taken to minimize vibrations when the demolition is carried out so as to reduce the environmental burdens of dust and noise and prevent cracks from developing in nearby buildings.

The first step therefore is gutting the house, which in the case of a one-family dwelling of this size will involve a team of approximately five men who will have to work between three and five days to prepare everything for the second phase, the actual demolition.

After this, the removal of the house will be carried out by a group of three men, including a foreman who will operate the excavator, as well as two helpers who will assist during the removal by using hand tools to break off smaller pieces that have gotten jammed, along with further wood or metal materials, and sorting them into the appropriate dumpsters. These two assistants must additionally maintain a steady spray of water to keep the dust to a minimum. This latter group will work for approximately a week and a half. Their most important tool is the so-called hydraulic excavator, a piece of equipment weighing between 20 and 25 tons with maximum 9 meters extension using an arm driven by a hydraulic cylinder. This excavator will begin with the removal of the house starting with the attic using a grapple attachment whose jaws are left slightly ajar so that the attic beams can be individually grasped and deposited directly in the dumpster reserved for wood, while the smaller bits of rubble are sifted out and fall to the ground.

After this the walls will be torn apart piece by piece working from above to below either continuing to use the grapple or else substituting a bucket attachment depending on the situation, and the debris deposited in the appropriate dumpster. The bucket attachment is an open piece of equipment that is primarily used for loading smaller materials or tearing out the foundation, but it can also, for example, be used to pull down a wall that has remained standing.

This house with a length of approximately 14 meters, a width of approximately 8 and a height of one and a half stories plus cellar, that is, of approximately 8 meters, comprises an enclosed space of approximately 900 cubic meters, which multiplied by 0.25 corresponds to 225 cubic meters of material. In order to calculate the number of truckloads that will be required to remove the debris, one must also take into account the fact that the material is not densely packed, which involves multiplying by a factor of 1.3. For this house, then, we can expect a loosely packed mass of approximately 290 cubic meters. Considering that each truckload can remove between 17 and 18 cubic meters of material, it will require approximately 17 trips with the tractor-trailer to transport all the material to one of the many construction rubble collection areas found in the region outside Berlin. Water has a density of 1, wood of 0.25, and brick rubble is estimated as 2.2. These are the respective figures for calculating tonnage. As a matter of principle the weight can be derived from the fixed bulk. The weight of the bathing house, which has no cellar (length 5.5 meters, width 3.8 meters), whose outer walls and interior fittings are made entirely of wood, therefore comprises only a scant 4 tons, while the weight of the main house is approximately 500 tons.

For a period of two weeks, first five men and then three are at work on the property. They stop for breakfast between 9 and 9:30 a.m., and for lunch between 12:00 noon and 1:00. During their breaks, the men sit on the grass to eat or drink, some of them lean against one or the other tree and smoke, looking out at the lake. When they are finished tearing down the house and only a pit remains to mark the place where it once stood, the property suddenly looks much smaller. Until the time comes when a different house will be built on this same spot, the landscape, if ever so briefly, resembles itself once more.

Acknowledgments

For their financial support that helped with the research and the writing of this book, I am grateful to Indra Wussow, Beate Puwalla, the Berliner Senat and the Robert Bosch Foundation.

For giving me access to a large number of documents and letters as well as film material and photographs that played a central role in my work, I would like to thank: Frau Dr. Diekmann of the Moses-Mendelssohn-Zentrum Potsdam; Frau Vespermann of LISUM Berlin; Frau Pohland of the Kreisarchiv Landkreis Oder-Spree; Frau Wagner of the Bundesarchiv; Frau Kandler of the Brandenburgisches Landeshauptarchiv; Frau Dr. Schroll of the Landesarchiv Berlin; Mr. Jagielski of the Jewish Historical Institute in Warsaw; and the Bauaktenarchiv Köpenick.

For assisting me in my research as well as offering ideas, advice and answers to a great many questions, I would like to thank: Dr. Weißleder, Andreas Peter, Ellen Jannings, Christel Neubelt-Minzlaff, Elisabeth Engel, Sascha Lewin, Gottlieb Kaschube, Irmgard Fischer, Botho Oppermann, Marga Thomas, Bernd and Angela Andres, Bernd Andres senior and Juttadoris Andres, Herr and Frau Benke, Rainer Wagner, Marion Welsch, the Müller-Huschke family, Dr. Faber, Karla Mindach, Herr Mindach, Reinhard Kiesewetter, Hans-O. Finke, Herr Herfurth, Jens Nestvogel, Frank Lemke, Dr. Zaumseil, Herr Torzinski, Dr. Alexander, Klaus Wessel, Dirk Erpenbeck, Anke Otten, Eliza Borg, Frau Erdmann, Rüdiger and Sigrid Galuhn, along with my father and mother.

For listening, and for his infinite patience with all the questions that without him I would only have been able to ask myself, I wish to thank Wolfgang.

'Oppressive, charming, scary ...
Jenny Erpenbeck is the rising star
of the German literary scene'

'Erpenbeck will get under your skin'

By the side of a lake in Brandenburg, a young architect builds the house of his dreams – a summerhouse with wrought-iron balconies, stained-glass windows the colour of jewels, and a bedroom with a hidden closet, all set within a beautiful garden. But the land on which he builds has a dark history of violence that began with the drowning of a young woman in the grip of madness, and that grows darker still over the course of the century. The Jewish neighbours disappear one by one; the Red Army requisitions the house, burning the furniture and trampling the garden; a young East German attempts to swim his way to freedom in the West; a couple return from brutal exile in Siberia and leave the house to their granddaughter, who is forced to relinquish her claim to it and sell it to new owners intent upon demolition.

With this haunting evocation of a home and its buried secrets, Jenny Erpenbeck peels back layer after layer of German history to reveal the beating heart and unique memories that lie beneath.